LAST CENTURY

It was a frenetic land undergoing an economic boom, but also an isolated outpost for lost souls.

Anything was possible — fortunes, visions, and the challenges of becoming a man.

Ron Morris applies the discipline of the short story to true tales of adventure: hiding from the Khmer Rouge, fired on during Thailand's Black May, beset by ghosts in the city, entombed with a legendary sword in Burma, living under Siamese skies...

Ta Prohm Temple, Cambodia

LAST CENTURY

BEING

THE TALES OF AN ADVENTURER IN
THE ASIAN TIGER ERA

RON MORRIS

New York: Villefort

New York: Villefort

Copyright © 2020 Ron Morris
Ingram edition 2025 ISBN: 978-1-939270-17-7

Also available as ebook ISBN: 978-1-939270-03-0

1 2 7 8 9 10 8 8 8 9

Cover design: Arnaud Romilly
Cover layout: Thiearapong Sereethanavong
Cover layout for 2025 Ingram edition:
Jatupol Kesornsukhon
and Ratha Titipattarananon
Photos: Ron Morris

Media enquiries: 2bangkok@gmail.com; ron@nortrad.com

Villefort Publishing
1325 Sixth Avenue, 28th Floor
New York, New York
10019

FOR MY PARENTS, RON B. AND FAYE ANN,
WHO SENT ME OUT INTO THE WORLD

Midway upon the journey of our life
  I found myself within a forest dark,
  For the straightforward pathway had been lost.
    The Divine Comedy, Inferno, **Dante Alighieri**

CONTENTS

NEW WORLD

IT was the decade of the Asian Tigers. With few exceptions, most Southeast Asian nations were hopeful junior members. Construction cranes lined the horizons. Buildings were hurled into the air by workers laboring all night. New affluence challenged every tradition. There was not a moment to spare.

I had left the fading New World and found an even newer one. It was a place far away, isolated and warm, where one could walk and be alone, even in the city, cocooned by the whirring sounds of mysterious languages and signs that could not be read. These were places where, if one took a wrong step and died, there would be no one to claim the body.

I thought I would discover the future of prosperity that was finally due—a thrilling new potential. This could set me apart. Surely hoards of my generation would soon descend on Asia to compete with me once they heard. Few came, however, and it only seemed weird to them that I stayed there, far from home and hamburgers and sensible ways of living. Those of my age back in my country were already pairing off for a lifetime of nagging and salaried work. I did not want to be seen to fail, so I stayed in the new world and tried to live.

The days passed and I lost sense of time. Years were counted out in a foreign script and stretched back to the birth of the Buddha. It was a bracing chaos that was tough to leave — insular cultures, strange violence, isolation and dreams.

It was my first decade being a grown up. I would make the right decision. I would decide what was real. I would go to a new place and make something happen, but exactly what, I did not know. Something would happen there, good or bad. Something would happen.

AT THE DISCO

ELECTRICITY had not been fully restored in Phnom Penh. A small generator chugged away outside the hotel and a single orange extension cord ran from the generator into the dark lobby.

I dragged along my battered suitcase. I did not want to be seen using a backpack, as I associated backpackers with no-good hippies who flitted about the region wearing flip flops and jumping from teaching job to teaching job.

A boy was waiting behind the desk at the hotel check-in. During that time, it seemed only the youngest people populated the city. Perhaps everyone older had been killed or otherwise exhausted by the years of war that had just passed.

The boy said, "Welcome to the Royal Hotel." It was a bright and cheery introduction for a dark and cavernous space. His grin appeared to be one of friendliness, but I knew that in this culture it could equally indicate unease.

After checking in, the boy, who introduced himself as Pich, led me away from the counter and through the empty lobby to a grand stairway to the upper floors. The floorboards occasionally creaked and popped as we walked along.

The upper floor hallways were dark, but open to the bright outside at both ends of the hall. The silhouette of a massive winged creature swooped down from the ceiling and then vanished back into the rafters.

"Bat," Pich said, as if it were an admirable feature of the hotel. He opened the door to my room before vanishing back into the hall.

The ceiling of my room was impossibly high in the dimness, like in the paneled drawing rooms and salons in old movies. Screened-in transoms topped the walls and allowed an occasional breeze from the nearby riverside to move through the building. The bathtub had great iron claw feet and the toilet tank was in the old style—high up on the wall with a long hanging chain to pull on to flush. Everything was worn but worked perfectly. I cannot recall exactly, but I think a room at the hotel was 36 U.S. dollars a night, a grand sum for Phnom Penh and for me at the time.

My room overlooked an open-air disco that was set up in a shaded courtyard in front of the hotel and took up the space between the hotel and the street. It was empty at midday. Rows of plastic tables and chairs, some large boxy speakers under a tarp, and Christmas lights strung overhead waited for the night.

This hotel, the Hotel Le Royal, was constructed in 1929 and once hosted luminaries such as Charlie Chaplin and W. Somerset Maugham. It was one of the grand dames of colonial-era travel, along with the Oriental in Bangkok, the Raffles in Singapore, and the Strand in Rangoon. It was the last stand of foreign journalists covering the fall of Phnom Penh to the Khmer Rouge in the 1970s. Some fled the city via the nearby Chroy Changvar Bridge, which was later mined and blown up by the Khmer Rouge in their fanatical campaign against the corrupt modernity of the world.

In Cambodia, history was not ancient. It was right there and the wound was open. Where usually history was hidden in black and white photos or committed by ancients who wore strange clothing, in Cambodia the epic battles and killings were fresh, committed just the other day against the very people I met.

There was some mystery in the name — Cambodia. It had a legendary sound to it like Mandalay or Zanzibar and was one of the world's extreme places. While the trajectory of Vietnam's years of war and eventual reunification was bloody, Cambodia was an outlying extreme of revolution. No doubt every nation has a clique of radicals who, mainly for rhetorical flair, express the belief that mass deaths must precede utopia, but such cabals are rarely able to gain control of government and then execute their desires for genocide and ruin. Cambodia, or "Kampuchea" as the Khmer Rouge preferred, became the endpoint of the human wreck that foreign powers unleashed by colonizing and then trying to hold on to the region.

Cambodia had dangerous and mysterious rebels who remained hidden beyond the ruins of the nation's once great ancient empire. This was where I wanted to go — to Angkor Wat. While the pyramids of Egypt were accessible at one of the world's crossroads, the mysterious Angkor kingdoms were buried in distant jungles.

To get to the Angkor ruins, I had to first go to the town of Siem Reap, but it was not possible to travel overland to Siem Reap then. The forests of the north and west were Khmer Rouge territory. Bridges and roads were impassible, and tales of danger from highwaymen and banditry were legion. The land was still heavily mined.

The only safe way to Siem Reap was the national airline, then flying only irregularly out of the nation's capital, Phnom Penh. To get a ticket, one had to fly to Phnom Penh, wait in line at the airline sales office, which started selling each day at 1:30 p.m., and pay cash for a roundtrip ticket to Siem Reap. This is what brought me to Phnom Penh.

Pich, the only person I ever saw at the hotel, presided over the hotel's front desk and kept it fastidiously clean and organized, with a battered but clean artificial fern and a few handwritten name cards for the hotel neatly arranged on the counter. This was a contrast to the rest of the shabby lobby. With his posture and demeanor, he was clearly trying to present the image of being a diligent professional. I also saw that he had a strangely furrowed brow for such a young person. It seemed to signify the agitated, resigned attitude of a person who had no choice but to get along in the situation he was in while covetously grasping for what he could get.

My own American presuppositions made me proud of him, as I judged that his hard work and dedication to his job would be their own reward and would somehow heal this place. It was a wish that everything would turn out well if everyone just tried hard.

He proudly wanted to know my opinion of his English skills and in return he gave me advice. He counseled me in worried terms about the dangers of the city.

"Don't trust the taxi! Don't trust the driver! Don't go far at night. Come back here. It's not safe. The people want money," he advised.

He picked out what he said was a taxi for me, but I never saw any actual taxis during the trip—only old cars and weathered drivers. Mine was a battered car piloted by a man who hung out in front of the hotel and was apparently a friend of Pich. Like most of the city dwellers I saw then, the man looked too young to be a taxi driver and had a drawn, almost pained expression on his face.

We rumbled through the streets of the city. Only the main streets were paved and the side streets were dirt. Many had large twisted trees standing out in the center of the road. A Thai friend later told me that 50 years earlier Bangkok was like this.

First I headed to a museum. The building was square-shaped with an open courtyard in the center. It had no electricity and was more warehouse than museum, with crates stacked up in the shadows. The air was moldy and still, and somewhere up in the rafters there was a continual rustling where hundreds of bats roosted. Gaps in ceiling were covered in wire, presumably to keep the animals from entering and roosting, but it did not work. A constant plinking sound from bat droppings and shafts of light from partially shuttered windows punctuated the darkness.

I walked through the museum, not being able to really see anything clearly. I was the only visitor. There were no labels or explanations — just stacks of mainly stone artifacts — broken nagas, Buddhas, and all manner of obscure items of decoration and worship that those of the past deemed necessary to create and those of the present deemed necessary to collect in this place. Bat debris continued to ping down, echoing in the dark like drops of water and giving the galleries an earthy, sharp smell.

A wiry and animated old man — I presumed he was a museum employee — followed me through the maze of crates. Suddenly he leapt up on a platform where several large, barrel-like objects were displayed. He explained they were ancient drums, hundreds of years old. They appeared to be made of thin metal and were covered with minute, fine decoration.

He urged me to pound on the ancient drum. I pretended I did not understand him, so he began beating on the drum. It gave off a thin thudding sound and the bats overhead shifted and more dust and debris rained down on my head. I thanked him and moved on.

At the airline ticket office, a line was already forming. It was less an office and more a room in a concrete shophouse, with only one worn table and a few chairs. I cannot recall how much the ticket price was, but I remember it had to be in exact change and in U.S. dollars only.

Those waiting were the odd, sometimes off-putting people who were the first to push out to see the new things there were to see at the ends of the world. An old frizzled-hair hippie man wore a 1970s-era cut-off t-shirt and shorts that were too short. An intense-looking man in corduroys stood alongside a blank-faced girl. A young man with a Jesus beard carried a guitar on his back. That type was in every backpacker crowd. Others looked like they were just trying not to be noticed.

An older German-speaking couple were wearing pith helmets and these were the first pith helmets I had ever seen outside of a movie. The couple looked like they should have been pottering around in their retirement gardens back home, but instead they were scouting out chaotic locations such as this.

In front of me in line was a musty smelling man of indeterminate age with a friendly smile, but haunted and vacant eyes.

"Do you know what the best beer in the world is?" he asked.

I mentioned the local brand — I cannot recall the name of it now. It was one of the few things widely advertised in the country then.

"No," he said. "Heineken. It's from my country. They will have it here soon." That seemed to be the totality of what he wanted me to know.

Behind me was the blank-faced girl. She carried a huge backpack. These oversized backpacks were once a common sight and a badge of honor for the extreme budget traveler in Asia.

The girl's eyes darted back and forth. "My father would never believe I am here," she said. "I'll probably end up getting raped." There was an element of maniacal resignation in her voice. She was not looking to see if I was shocked.

"It's true, you know," she continued.

We spoke of where we each came from and she became a bit more sensible the more she spoke.

"I grew up in Pennsylvania, but I hated it there and moved to California, then I went up to San Francisco. I hated everyone there too and then I decided to travel," she said.

Two locals entered, one carrying a small lockbox and the other several frayed pads of paper. Sitting at the table, they began to take money for the tickets to Siem Reap and write out, by hand, both the receipt and the ticket. The line started moving.

A number of steps were required in the ticket-buying process. This necessitated signing something, getting a form, filling it out and returning to the line again. Everyone was kept busy filling out and signing and waiting in line. A surprising number of stamps were employed to make the papers official, and the ticket sellers seemed to relish the authority they were conferring with their loud stamping. The stamps they used were so old that the resulting stamp was a smudgy blur, but everything was stamped and stamped again and initialed and signed, and the money duly collected and stacked neatly in the lockbox.

Finally, I had my handwritten airline ticket. The ticket agents collected their stamps and prepared to leave, even as more people were arriving to buy tickets. I noticed that the ticket sellers had no identification, but I guessed they were genuine. Only a genuine ticket seller would dare show up with no ID, take everyone's money, and then leave while more bemused customers were arriving.

The blank-faced girl left, as did the man with the haunted eyes, the German couple, and the Jesus guitarist. Then I left. All moving on.

At a nearby roundabout, piles of rubble lined the road and a cluster of electricity poles were covered with photos of people being searched for—people lost in the previous years of chaos. Some of these posters were printed by the United Nations, but others were homemade. A few showed childhood photos with several siblings hugging, but most were the Asian-style ID photos showing a serious-looking young man or woman, now lost, scattered by the years of revolution. The flyers fluttered in the hot sun. There was no one else on the street. I felt the need to look at every photo, and I did so while wondering what had become of each person.

The Tuol Sleng Genocide Museum was one of the must-see tourist sites in the town. It was a former school that was converted into a detention and torture center by the Khmer Rouge. After the war, the site was again transformed, this time into a museum to document the abuses of the Khmer Rouge. Guides, who I was informed witnessed the actual events, led me through the classrooms, explaining the macabre details, like how barbed wire was strung along the exterior walkways outside the classrooms. This prevented detainees from hurling themselves off the balconies to die voluntarily, rather than waiting for their deaths by torture.

Throughout were crude paintings that illustrated the atrocities, such as one in which hundreds of detainees were shackled together in a room. Another showed Khmer Rouge soldiers throwing babies into the air to shoot them or impale them on spikes. One room displayed the now famous wall of photos of the detainees — their torture and death meticulously documented by their tormentors.

Last on the tour was a row of special interrogation cells, each with a single metal bed. These were used to torture confessions out of high-level detainees, most of whom were members of the Khmer Rouge who had fallen out of favor.

My guide claimed he was one of only a few people who was an inmate and had survived. He explained in detail the torture that went on in the room — the beatings, the electric shocks — and claimed the red stains on the floor were the original blood, but it clearly looked like red paint to me.

Like Cambodia at the time, Tuol Sleng had a utilitarian aspect that hinted that these events had only recently happened and that the suffering was fresh. Every part of the site urgently conveyed the message that ultimately people could be made to be disposable. It was easy to see that in this post-revolutionary era there was danger as well. It was a heaviness of many things past that could run down and crush a person.

There was nothing distinctive about the place. It was a series of cement classrooms festooned with barbed wire and folksy signs explaining the terrible activities that once went on there. Yet it was the only place I have ever visited, before or since, that had its own mood. It was like entering a heavy cube of black fog that sat on the site. It was not menacing, but more like a distant desperation. It lingered around me all the time I was there.

The guide ended the tour in the last interrogation room with a metal bed and the red substance on the floor.

"Why did they do this? No reason!" he ended in a practiced and dramatic way, but also with real emotion.

As I exited the room, I was surprised to see my taxi driver standing near the door, watching me and the guide. Once we were back in the taxi, he leaned conspiratorially to me and spat out angrily, "No, not true, none of this is true! Lies!"

I did not know he could speak my language and I asked him to explain, but he refused to say anything more.

In the evening, I walked down the street from my hotel, not straying too far in the darkness after Pich's earlier warnings. The city was stealthy and quiet, like a brooding countryside.

Only a few shops were open on each street. These were neighborhood stores in two-storey shophouses, in which a family lived in the upstairs part and ran a shop downstairs. Every item in these shops was imported from Thailand.

Since there was no dependable electricity, each shophouse had its own roaring generator out in front on the sidewalk, with a power cable running inside, just like at the hotel. The generators spat out exhaust, and a pall of bluish smoke hung over every street. The shops with generators were pools of light, dropped randomly here and there in the otherwise dark streets. In between it was pitch black. The storm drains were uncovered for some unknown reason, so I had to be careful moving through the darkened areas to avoid falling in.

In front of each shop stood an armed guard—invariably a young boy with a battered rifle or AK-47. They were oddly uniform—young boys, guns slung jauntily across their backs and every one delighted to see a foreigner and ask him in incredibly broken English where he was from and what he thought of Cambodia.

I bought some cans of Coke from one of the shops. Cambodia had yet to inaugurate a new currency and was using the U.S. dollar in the meantime. I was interested to find that even the change was in U.S. coins, imported in bulk to provide the country a complete currency during the U.N. administration period.

Incredibly, one boy guard held what looked like a grenade launcher, complete with a cone-shaped projectile on its end. I wondered how this might be used in the event of a robbery. I imagined a shoplifter being hit with a grenade.

Standing there as blue smoke wafted around me, standing so close to such a lethal weapon, I did not appreciate the danger, but instead was almost giddy to be in such a free and out-of-control location.

A U.N. Japanese peacekeeper arrived and tried to explain to the boy that if he shot his grenade weapon off in the enclosed area of the street, he would likely blow himself up as well.

This jarred me back to reality and I hurried away quickly. There was a fine line between having a great anecdote to tell and getting blown up.

Later, I learned that the arriving U.N. soldiers quickly gathered up the guns and prohibited the young guards from standing openly on the street, so it was lucky I was able to see that at all.

In a first, the United Nations was attempting to administer an entire country. The United Nations Transitional Authority in Cambodia (UNTAC) was managing all the activities of government. I was particularly intrigued to meet both Japanese and German peacekeepers, as it was one of the first times these nations permitted their military to serve overseas since World War II. The peacekeepers wore baseball caps with a distinctive emblem above the brim with the mission's logo on it. I asked some of the peacekeepers to give or sell one to me, but no one would.

The only area where I saw foreigners congregating was in a cluster of small outdoor restaurants. Driving by, I noticed a fat older man sitting by the roadside with a young girl on his lap and several other girls nearby. At the time, nothing registered in my mind about what must have been going on. It was only years later that I realized this was evidence of the rampant sex trafficking of young girls that the region became known for. So in this far place, there were men whose anxious desires prompted them to take advantage of the most vulnerable peoples in the world. In this place, their abuse might even seem to those reestablishing the peace to be a lesser problem compared to the re-creation of an entire nation.

In the evening, I walked over to the Tonle Sap River that ran through the city. The opposite bank was overgrown and nearly empty. A mere 20 years later, the far side would be completely developed with hundreds of buildings hugging the river, but on that day, the ruined Chroy Changvar Bridge stood broken at the riverside, yearning for the other side. Its middle sections were gone, deliberately blown up, but the approaches from either side were still standing defiantly — or pathetically — now a monument to the purging madness of the Khmer Rouge.

Back in my hotel room, I sat and listened. The tops of the walls and hallways in the hotel were screened in so that air could circulate freely. I never heard any sound from another room nor saw any other guests in the hotel. A fresh musty odor moved through. I did not know for sure, but I guessed that this was from the presence of the fruit bats hanging in the high ceilings of the hallways. It was pleasing to catch a glimpse of them and hear them rustling in the night.

I fell asleep.

Much later in the night, the tinny thumping of music from the disco in the forecourt of the hotel woke me up.

I opened the shutters to the balcony and peered down at the young people milling around, some dancing, some drinking around a beer keg. Christmas lights blinked randomly above them. For some time, half awake, I listened to the music.

As with all music played over speakers in Asia, it sounded to me a bit too loud — almost to distortion — and overly rich in treble. When the elders of my own culture would be saying "Turn it down!" it seems the Cambodians would be saying "Turn it up!" and "Have fun!"

The song was in a foreign tongue, Khmer, I assumed, and it was sung in a young girl's clear, sharp and joyous voice from an earlier age before the years of destruction, sung at a time before war when the engaging nonsense of popular music and celebrity could be enjoyed and regarded as an important thing.

I wondered if the singer ever guessed that someday her nation would consume itself and that every normal part of her culture would become a thing of fear to be smashed away. Maybe she was one of the many singers and actors rounded up and liquidated by the Khmer Rouge to enable the ushering in of their golden age of history starting with Year Zero. This voice from a happier time could mean that the good times — the normal times — would come again.

Songs continued, one merging into another in the night.

Then, from every side, uniformed men rushed into the disco. The crowd on the dance floor fell back, screaming and shouting. Then it was suddenly silent. The apparent leader of the uniformed men stepped forward and spoke with authority. He was both arrogant, knocking some bottles off a table for effect, as well as officious. There was another pause, as if something was asked of those at the disco, but no one answered. Then a melee erupted, with the uniformed men grabbing the young men and forcibly dragging them away. Others who could, fled in all directions.

One of the last boys carried away twisted to escape the grasp of the soldiers and I saw it was Pich. I do not think he saw me, or that anyone noticed me, for that matter, but Pich suddenly began screaming in English, "Help! Help!"

It was a proud and strained voice, as if each word of the foreign tongue forced his voice higher until Pich was yelping like an animal caught in a trap, wailing about his fate.

Every table and chair was upturned, girls screamed and a few punches were thrown, but the captured young men were soon put into trucks at the street side.

Then the trucks pulled away and there was no one left at the disco. The ground was littered with broken plastic chairs, bottles of beer and dozens of flip flops that had fallen off the boys' feet as they were dragged off. It was a sad peace. Then the power went out and the disco and hotel vanished in the darkness.

I rushed out of my room and quickly felt my way down the stairs to the lobby, stumbling over several steps in the shadowy, empty space.

Outside on the street, the power generator for the hotel was gone as well, likely taken by the uniformed men. It was black and still and I thought of the unimaginable things that must be happening just out of my view.

A soldier materialized, turning suddenly out of the black to face me as if he had been there all along. He was uncomfortably close and I was startled. I blurted out, "What happened?"

I instantly realized he probably did not understand me, but also that I should not have let on that I had witnessed anything. I should not have run out into this out-of-control place at night.

He looked at me with a surprising thoughtfulness and then paused, as if he were finding the right words. Then he licked his lips and carefully said, with practically no accent, "For army."

His expression changed to one of expectation. Had I understood? Was I appreciative of his English-language acumen?

"Ah, thank you," I said.

The soldier beamed.

I turned and retreated into the safety of the bat-filled hotel.

The next morning nothing had changed. No electricity. Bats rustled in the hall. Looking down from my room, the disco was the same. Overturned bottles and chairs glistened in the morning sunlight.

I already felt a growing claustrophobia. I could not wait to get out of the uncertainty of Phnom Penh. I was going to be heading to where the Khmer Rouge was still fighting in the northwest. It had buried itself deep in the jungle, near the twelfth-century ruins of Angkor Wat.

I also felt as if I should do something right then. I should find out what had happened and what would happen next. But I already knew. There was unseen suffering and I knew it was going on.

The front desk was set as if Pich had just stepped out for a moment. His satchel and lunch pail were waiting behind the counter.

I left.

At the airport I spoke to a Japanese U.N. peacekeeper — more were appearing by the hour — telling him what had happened at the hotel disco.

"That's the... draft. They are not supposed to do that," he said with a little smile.

THE STILL FOREST

THERE was very little to be seen from the air. It was an endlessly empty land, not sectioned off into densely populated parcels as in nearby Thailand. Only a few people were on the plane and when I arrived at Siem Reap, the airport was deserted. I waited on the tarmac for my bags to be pulled out of the aircraft hold.

As if to compensate for the solitude, three massive tandem-rotor helicopters approached the airport from across the plains.

There was something transfixing about the choppers, hanging in the air while gradually growing larger and larger. The rhythmic deep thumping of the blades descended into a chaotic mixture of sound and pressure as they neared.

The first two landed, disgorging several dozen blue-uniformed U.N. soldiers, who were spreading out across Cambodia to administer the country. Moments later, the third chopper landed and only two people disembarked. They were an average-looking middle-aged Western couple, bickering intensely in a foreign language.

I took a taxi, which was really just an old car, from the airport into the town of Siem Reap, the modern town adjacent to the Angkor Wat area. The road into Siem Reap was a small pot-holed avenue that alternated between paved and unpaved. The driver made a point to stop and show me the "Siamese Defeated" monument. I remember it as a small concrete structure painted white at the juncture of three roads.

This monument was a reference to the apocryphal meaning of the town's name, Siem Reap. Some attributed the meaning to be "the Siamese defeated," to refer to an ancient battle when invading Siamese armies were thrown back. Other residents I met over the years believed it referred to the events of the early and mid-twentieth century when the Siamese state occupied and then had to abandon the northwest of present-day Cambodia, which included the Angkor Wat area.

On subsequent trips, I was unable to find this monument. Maybe it was removed or relocated when the Cambodians wanted to downplay their animosity towards the Thais who would later build hotels along the airport road into the city. I do not think I imagined it.

Siem Reap was an isolated outpost, only safely journeyed to by plane. Everything between the town and the Thai border to the west was the lair of the Khmer Rouge. They endured in their jungle stronghold that no world power had the ability or willingness to penetrate. They held a special place, even among genocidal regimes, for their fanatical destruction of their own people. Cities were emptied to return the nation to its presumed ideal agrarian state while those wearing eyeglasses were liquidated to stamp out the nation's intellectuals. Westerners, usually permitted to stand by and wring their hands while witnessing war and revolution, were also captured by the Khmer Rouge, tortured into writing confessions and executed. There were no diplomatic niceties in the Khmer Rouge's version of reality. Even a few unlucky foreigners blown off course after sailing from nearby Thailand were likewise consumed. Mass graves were still being discovered when I was first there, such as when bones protruded from a remote rice field or an abandoned gasoline supply tank was found stuffed with corpses.

To the east of Siem Reap was the realm of highwaymen and a landscape stripped of bridges and infrastructure by years of war. Even boat traffic on the Tonle Sap inland sea to the south was subject to banditry.

At the edge of the town, concrete block buildings stood around randomly — a small warehouse, a deserted gas station. Once part of some greater world, they were now shuttered or open to dust and vine — maybe places where people died for no good reason.

The city was an eerily still place, as if waiting for something bad to happen, but it represented hope that a rational government could restore control over formerly lawless areas of the country.

I was driven around a central square and a small park. On the north side was the Grand Hotel d'Angkor, an edifice that harked back to the era of genteel travel by wealthy foreigners who arrived by ocean liner in Bangkok and journeyed across the plains to Angkor. It was boarded up, awaiting the foreign investment that would resurrect it in future years.

At that time, the Grand Hotel d'Angkor was one of the few buildings between the town and the ruins, but today the five kilometers beyond it are entirely developed, nearly to the edge of the Angkor area.

There were no proper hotels in Siem Reap then. Instead many shophouses had a converted upstairs room for the occasional tourist to stay in.

I do not recall how I knew about the place where I was planning to stay, but I did have the address when I arrived in Siem Reap and the driver found the location without any problem. We pulled up to a four-storey shophouse.

The door was slightly open, so I entered. Inside, it was the darkened foyer of a home. I called out, but apparently no one was there, so I sat down in a chair and slowly dozed off.

I was roused by a girl. "You!" she said. It sounded like a form of greeting, like saying, "Hey!"

Whether she had just arrived or was somewhere else in the house all along, I could not tell, but lights were now on and some indeterminate food was cooking somewhere inside.

I was led up to my room on the fourth floor via a series of stairways. These steep stairways were common in the concrete shophouses of modern Asia. Throughout the house, tables, chairs and cabinets were situated where they should be, but there were few extraneous possessions and nothing on the clean, painted walls. A return to capitalism after years of communism had not yet afforded the opportunity to amass the bric-a-brac that cluttered homes elsewhere.

The girl's name was Rotha. I later learned she was 21, but she looked years younger, deliberate and utilitarian in her movements, as only those who have to work hard from a young age are.

My room had no door. It was just a space at the top of the stairs. My room key was the key to the house itself. I was shown a bed and then warned, in the gravest terms, not to go out at night on foot, by bicycle or car.

"It is not safe in this town," she said to me, as blankly as if she were speaking in a trance. She told me that the electricity would soon go off and then left me alone.

I peered out the window. It was made of small rectangles of glass deeply beveled so that only a small square of each pane afforded a clear view. It was already dim outside and the street was empty.

The extensive ruins I wanted to visit were north of the town. Angkor Wat was the most striking and singular of these. It was a collection of fantastical towers in an otherworldly style with dense ornamentation, evoking the look of Hindu temples. Beyond Angkor Wat was the walled city of Angkor Thom. During the 1200s, hundreds of thousands lived there. Now it was a maze of jungle ruins.

Massive moats and reservoirs had enabled the ancient Angkorian world to master the waters unleashed by seasonal monsoons. This had allowed multiple rice crops in a single year, without having to rely on the cycles of wet and dry seasons to provide the standing water needed for cultivation.

I sat down on the bed, thinking about this haunted place and what I might find. Somewhere in the house was a clock that chimed on the hour. It was a deep, momentous-sounding chime and it kept me awake at first.

The next day, I entered the ancient city. Most of its waterways were filled in with centuries of debris. Some areas of the moats outside of Angkor Wat had collections of huts standing where water once was. There were no trappings of modern-day tourism — no trash cans, bathrooms, or souvenir stands. Nothing framed the ruins as being a managed attraction. They were only stones, enduring in the sun.

I did not see any of the foreigners who were in Phnom Penh earlier buying tickets to Siem Reap. The only foreigners I saw at Angkor Wat were an Indian delegation of eight people accompanied by armed guards. They seemed perplexed to see me walking around alone.

"Be careful," one member of the delegation told me.

"You shouldn't be here," another whispered to me.

The tableau of stone temples was underscored by a constant muffled thumping in the distance. This was the Khmer Rouge shelling in the next province. The sound eventually took on a soothing, thunder-like quality, but it was clearly artillery of some kind, and its sound prevented any sense of true serenity.

Along the outside walls of Angkor Wat were stone carvings depicting the battles, mythology and environment of the ancient culture. Certain parts depicting kings, gods or potent animals like elephants had been rubbed for good fortune by generations of people. This continual touching, and presumably the impregnation of sweat and oils from people's hands, had converted the sandstone into a jet-black, gleaming, marble-like stone. This made the gods, kings and elephants stand out in obsidian luster from the rest of the carvings. In later years, ropes would be set up in front of these areas to prevent further touching.

My most prominent memory of Angkor Wat is the persistent smell of urine that wafted on the breeze throughout its corridors.

The colossal permanence of the temple had made it an occasional shelter for those rendered homeless by war or flooding. The stains of human habitation — urination and walls stained by cooking fires — were obvious throughout the complex.

In just a few years, tourism would cease for a time and Angkor Wat would be a temporary home to over 5000 refugees. The refugees would be seeking shelter from the Khmer Rouge that had once again infiltrated the province to demonstrate that they remained a consequential force.

Outside of Angkor Wat, the more far-flung ruins were ringed by signs warning of mines. As I was exiting the terraced pyramid-like ruins of Ta Keo, two U.N. peacekeepers, the first I had seen in the area, frantically called to me from the road, shouting that the temple had not yet been demined and that there should have been warning signs set up there.

After spending the rest of the day visiting ruins in the surrounding area, I returned to Angkor Wat at twilight. Earlier, a few monks had been walking around (along with the Indian delegation), but now it was empty.

With every waft of air that flowed through the temple, the urine smell arose and combined with the deep smell of earth. With each step, this earthy smell awoke in the dark.

Every stone was black. The sky and jungle were the darkest blue. There was no source of light, but between the black and the near black of the sky, I was able to wander about, feeling my way down the corridors, careful not to stumble over the raised thresholds of each chamber or slip on the many oddly spaced and worn steps that extended in every direction. It was quiet and I was invisible in its vastness.

Centuries and unknown history had expelled millions who once lived in the area and filled up the moats that generations had worked so hard to create. War and revolution had emptied the modern town of Siem Reap and what remained were its shuttered buildings and its unsafe streets.

Being clever, defiantly clever, is the province of the untempered young. I thought to myself with satisfaction, "How far away I am...

how alone." I wanted to be far away from slights and judgments of the future. I thought that I was the only wise man.

After dwelling on this for a moment, I put it out of my mind as I scrambled through the black hallways and down the steep stairs in a moonless night I could never have imagined before this day.

The next morning, I realized how mosquito-bitten I was. I also was badly sunburned around my neck. Rotha, who I passed on the way out of the shophouse in the morning, looked shocked as she saw the sunburn and suggested I should go to the hospital for treatment, but I ignored the pain.

That day I went to Ta Prohm. This was the one temple that had been left in the same state as when it was rediscovered in the nineteenth century, overcome with vegetation.

On the way to the site, I asked the driver what wildlife lived in the forest and the driver said there was none. According to him, throughout the years of war, soldiers in their hunger had scoured the landscape, eating all that there was to eat, consuming every squirrel, rat, insect, and anything that could be skewered and grilled or boiled.

It was a long distance from the dirt road into the forest to Ta Prohm, and, during the walk, a flock of squawking parrots zoomed overhead. They, at least, had escaped being consumed.

Unlike most of the other temples that were cleared of vegetation and stood in the sun, Ta Prohm was under a forest of spectacular trees and covered in dappled shade. The stones that formed the buildings and walls were covered with dark lichen and electric green moss.

Giant trees grew where seeds had fallen on temple roofs. Their massive, shiny roots draped over the tops of the temples, sometimes causing the structures to collapse. The trees presided over the resulting piles of stones, roots grasping them like a snake holding its prey. Inside the remaining structures, long temple hallways ended abruptly in massive piles of stones where the roof and walls had collapsed, blocking the way. I witnessed a solitary day at the temple. It was one place in the world that no one else had bothered to visit that day.

In the late afternoon, I went south to the great inland sea of Tonle Sap. The driver was a man who had lost part of his lower leg to a landmine.

Just outside of town were empty dirt roads leading in many directions. Vines reached out, narrowing most of the roads to mysterious trails going to some unknown place.

The twisting stream alongside the dirt road that led to Tonle Sap was lined with hundreds of homemade water wheels. The road became ever rougher until the car could go no further, and I walked the last kilometer to the inland sea. The dirt of the road had been trodden into a talcum-powder consistency and it drifted up into the brightness.

It was the dry season, and the inland sea of Tonle Sap had receded as it did every year, leaving only a small tributary up to the village that would have been at the shoreline during the rainy season. The place stank of sewage and rotting fish and was little more than a group of huts on a mud flat waiting for the seasonal waters to return. As I was leaving the village, a boat motored into view and a man threw a grenade or some sort of small explosive device into some huts clustered on the muddy shore. Walls blew down and a flame shot up as people screamed and scattered. I fled through the dust and the sun back to the car.

That evening, I returned to my odd hotel. The layout of the place was confusing, and at times I heard people moving about on the lower floors, and at other times, the house was empty and dark.

I decided to talk to Rotha, but when I ventured downstairs, the house was deserted. Then I went back up to my room and fell asleep for a moment, but then there she was, standing at the top of the stairs. I could hear the sounds of others downstairs and again smelled the indistinct odor of something cooking.

"Hi," I said.

"Did you want something? Is everything ok?" she said, as if I had summoned her.

"No, I just..." I awkwardly segued into a recounting of my adventures and trying to invite her to come with me. It was probably something like, "It's really fantastic" and "Have you been?"

I thought she might want to come along with me the next day, when I intended to visit the Bayon and other places in the inner city of Angkor Thom. I imagined that she would want to accompany a dashing foreigner like me into the jungle.

"I'm going there tomorrow. Do you want to come too?" I asked.

She was entirely blank and uninterested in what I was saying. A Westerner typically adopts what we consider a smiling and friendly face in such situations in an attempt to elicit some likewise friendly face in response. There was nothing coming back to me.

The clock that I never saw chimed its deep chime.

"I can't go," she said with finality.

"Ok," I said. "Good night."

She said nothing more and left. I was never good at stuff like that.

There was only one thing related to the ruins on sale to tourists. The previous day, on my way to Ta Prohm, a tiny boy emerged from the forest with a single neatly bound and stapled copy of Henri Parmentier's *Guide to Angkor*, which I purchased for a dollar.

While modern guidebooks make definitive statements about what the monuments were meant to mean, this early guide, written by one of the first Europeans to systematically document the area, is more circumspect in its judgments, leaving perhaps a more accurate picture of what is actually known about the civilization that created the stone metropolis.

What little the taxi drivers who ferried me around could tell me, I suspected to be modern-day urban legends, such as that acrobats walked on wires stretched between the Prasat Suor Prat towers in Angkor Thom or that Angkor Wat was aligned with the pyramids in Egypt. *Guide to Angkor* was an antidote to these tales about a place that was still being prised from the jungle.

At the center of the walled city of Angkor Thom was the Bayon. It was particularly unusual, not only for its apparent mixture of Buddhist and Hindu influence combined with the royal cult of King Jayavarman VII, but also for being built awkwardly over and around a previous temple, parts of which could clearly be seen from within the existing structure. Monumental heads, 216 in all, look out from many directions and levels of the temple's towers. The faces have a hint of a Buddha-like smile, self-satisfied at being able to preside over the people who enter the temple grounds after all these centuries. It is believed that the Buddha faces were made to resemble the visage of King Jayavarman VII. This presumably created a temple that combined the god-cult of King Jayavarman VII with Theravada Buddhist and Hindu influences. Whatever it really was meant to mean, the Bayon was unique, even for Angkor.

It was to be my last day among the ruins and I rose early, before dawn, to be at the Bayon.

The driver did not show up as scheduled, so I was driven around by a young boy in a large American car with no windshield. The pedals of the car had a bundle of something — it looked like rags — strapped to them so he could press them.

I arrived while it was dark. A few other vehicles were there already, but I did not see any tourists. The smell of the damp earthy forest was still strong before the sunrise. The Bayon was surrounded by tall trees, and mist crept out of the forest and wrapped the black smiling towers in a haze. I noticed the strange silence. The distant shelling had ceased and even the birds were quiet. I walked the hundred meters to the temple from where the vehicles were parked.

All the temples at Angkor, just like those in neighboring Thailand and Myanmar, have a raised threshold that one steps over when entering each room. Various folk and religious traditions say spirits reside in the thresholds and thus one should step over without touching them out of respect. It is awkward to the modern-day person, who expects to step on the threshold, but it reminds one that you are entering a new, specific space bordered and protected by spirits. Whether these beliefs existed 900 years ago, I did not know, but I stepped over the heavily worn threshold and entered the precincts of the Bayon.

The stones were much darker than those in other temples, and overhead from a tower, I spied one of the massive faces of Jayavarman VII looking down at me. Then, from another angle, another identical face looked on. As I went forward, more faces emerged from different angles and levels to observe me. Puddles of water were everywhere, further multiplying the stone faces.

High walls stood among piles of rubble, and partially collapsed halls created a maze. I ventured up to the middle levels of the complex while the light gently increased and the slight fog dissipated.

Suddenly, the sound of gunfire erupted. First it was a vague popping like a firecracker, then intermixed with a sharper and more present rat-a-tat-tat. Then absolute silence. I was transfixed, listening. It seemed as if a long time was passing. I wondered why those sounds were so nearby.

In an instant, everything sprang to life again. Outside the temple on the road, the waiting drivers ran to their vehicles and all (including my driver) drove away at high speed, leaving me alone.

More firing erupted, much closer now, and I heard yelling and then cheering from the forest near where the vehicles had been parked. Armed men started to spill out from several points of the surrounding forest. I immediately ducked down from where I was visible on the upper terraces of the temple. I could tell the men were not regular government soldiers. During those days, the Khmer Rouge would sometimes make a foray into the symbolically important Angkor Wat area. This is what I was witnessing.

So there I was. I had gone too far after all. I told myself it was not the time to be scared. There was only the thing that needed to be done now. I did not dare to leave the temple, as I would surely be seen. I climbed back down into the lower, partially ruined parts. I headed to an area that was built on top of the walls of an earlier structure. This created peculiar spaces where the newer sections of the temple were built above the old sections. Modern concrete supports as well as collapsed sections further added to the confusion. There, I reasoned I would be able to find a crevice to hide in and then hope that the fighters did not hold the area for long.

As I neared the place where I thought I could best hide, an ear-splitting sound of celebratory gunfire burst from the other side of the wall, along with a volley of hearty, but tired sounding, cheers. This was too close.

I wedged myself into a space in the wall. Then, frightened by the ever-nearing sounds of men marching, I repositioned myself in another space nearby. This was not a wise move. Once I had settled into the new space, I found I was partially facing an open door to my left where the armed men began to march by outside of the temple. They were wearing the distinctive Khmer checkered scarves common among villagers in the country. I knew they must be followers of Pol Pot, the Khmer Rouge leader who was living deep in the festering forests to the west.

Most of the men were carrying packs and bundles, but some were carrying guns and metal ammunition boxes. It was an arresting sight. I froze and tried to become like the stones and melt into my surroundings. If becoming invisible was possible, I wanted it to happen at that moment. The men marched. There were many of them — too many.

They were not entering the temple yet. This must be a good sign. They must be just moving through. Surely if they were going to hold the area, they would set up camp in this stone fortress.

One of the men stopped abruptly and stood in the doorway of the temple. He was looking through the entryway as if he knew someone was there, but dared not step over the enchanted threshold and enter. I was just to the left of him and he could have easily seen me if he happened to look to his left, especially if I moved. I began to feel he must know I was there. I kept my eyes motionless and tried to still my mind.

I think he was young, but it was hard to tell. He looked hungry, almost haggard, but somehow robust, as if nothing could ever touch him. A fresh Khmer scarf framed his head of almost bushy black hair. Unlike most of the soldiers marching by, who were prominently carrying guns, he gave me the impression that he was a holy man — if such a thing was possible among the Khmer Rouge. He was vibrant and aware. He took off his scarf and held it deliberately with both hands as he stood before the doorway. The meaning of this, I never knew.

I imagined he had once been a city dweller who was forced into the jungle by the years of war. Maybe he was one of the idealistic comrades educated in France who returned to his home country with the hope to improve his nation by liquidating the bourgeoisie. As years passed in the jungle he had become attuned to the signals and sounds that came to him and he sensed something in this temple I was hiding in. He was uncompromising.

I felt he was studying the temple entryway suspiciously, as if deciding whether to enter. As soon as I thought this, he suddenly pulled around the rifle which was hanging at his back. He was poised to enter.

On the ground between us was a puddle and from the edge of my vision I could see him, almost head to toe, reflected in it. I thought he would certainly see me. I planned to run once this happened, but I would have to at least take a step towards him first to move out of the nook I was crouched in. It was not an ideal situation.

Waiting is a specific horror — waiting for big things to happen, for guns to go off, for events out of my control to grind by. I was waiting to see if something was going to fall on my head and change my life forever. In that moment, there was nothing to think of, no meaning to be had. There would be plenty of time to look back on this in terror later when all was safe.

Maybe the great stone faces, whatever they were really meant to be, were distracting him. I am sure he locked eyes with them as they loomed over us.

The longer it went on, the more I felt as if this soldier knew I was hiding inside. He was reaching out, probing, as if my presence was sending out a signal that I was there. I stilled my mind again.

The soldier continued to stand motionless, halted by the temple threshold, but reaching intently into the space to find me. Suspicion and surprise moved across his face in turn, as if he was using all his effort to detect whoever was inside.

Then a voice called out and he turned slightly to the right, away from my location. The spell was broken. He stepped back, almost reluctantly, and looked with resignation higher up at the temple towers, as if he now knew he would never discover what he was looking for. Then he was gone and the soldiers continued to march by.

I remained motionless, petrified, for a long time. The sounds of the men drifted away. Then there was a long expanse of silence when I was aware of how far away and alone I was in this place whose real purpose and meaning had been lost in the expanse of time.

The hesitant chirping of birds slowly grew and then even a breeze moved through the temple as the sun appeared over the tree tops.

The sound of returning vehicles finally roused me. When I peered out from the temple entrance, I saw the little kid who was my driver running up and gesturing to me to come quickly.

I rushed back to the car and returned to Siem Reap.

I let myself into the shophouse and went upstairs to my doorless room. The house was dark and quiet, and again it appeared no one was home. I stayed in my room for the rest of the day. The unseen clock bonged on every hour, but I was getting used to it.

That evening, I walked over to the Grand Hotel d'Angkor. It was empty and derelict, but on the back lawn was a makeshift restaurant. Homemade dishes were set out on old battered tables under three small bare light bulbs. In the gloom nearby, a few folding tables and chairs awaited diners. The food was good and filling and the night around was again deadly quiet.

I walked back in the darkness. The streets were empty except for a random motorcycle that sped by, maybe trying to get off the road as soon as possible. Something about the events of the day made me feel fearless. Surely nothing could touch me. Yet I was relieved to arrive back at the shophouse.

It was my last night. I said goodbye to this country and its anxious cities and tense ruins and history. I said goodbye to the unseen bonging clock. I never saw anyone in the house again.

It was another hot and still day when I left in the morning. While I was waiting for my flight at the airport, an agitated young man who I had never seen before found me and demanded I return the shophouse key.

I had neglected to leave it behind when I left the house. The key was attached to a chunk of wood, so it was incredible I had forgotten it, but I had. It was embarrassing and I am sure Rotha must have believed that I was purposely trying to run away with a souvenir. The young man took back the key and drove away on a noisy motorcycle.

Once in the air, I only saw the bright green below, as the plane tilted off into the sun.

QUACK PRACTITIONERS

WHENEVER I grasped my clipboard and was writing something down, there was a slight tremor in my hand. The owner of the business I worked at in Bangkok noticed this.

He first gave me a jar of herbal pills and said these were a cure for the tremor. I did not know what to say, so I just thanked him and said I would try them. They smelled like the incense that hangs in Chinese temples — a thick, laden, pungent flavor with no hint of sweetness.

I took a few of the tiny pills. They tasted like the Japanese herbal breath lozenges that once were popular in Asia, but that were now only used by old people. Although the label was in Thai, I could make out that no ingredients were listed. They tasted ok, but I thought there was no reason to take a chance that they contained something unhealthy, so I did not take any more.

A couple of weeks later, my boss told me he was bringing me and several of his Thai staff to see the doctor who invented the pills. The doctor would surely cure the tremor I had, I was told. Despite my reservations, I wanted to be a part of this. It was a different sort of medicine—an experience tinged with magic and old Siamese ways. My boss appeared pleased that he could offer me this special cure.

At every level of the Thai world, care was taken to ensure good fortune and proper alignment with the energies that control fate and reward goodness. This can range from following the cultural niceties of greeting others to stringent devotion to fringe cults. Thus it was probably no surprise that those claiming to know "the way," especially in relation to correcting what was wrong, were immediately believed without skepticism. Patients offer awe and the practitioner reflects it, offering hope that something good could happen.

I had long heard Western hippies extolling the superior wisdom of the East and its traditional cures that were spurned by greedy corporations that wanted to prescribe expensive drugs. Maybe this doctor could help me.

When we arrived, the place immediately struck me as strange—an average-looking shophouse in a dead-end alley near Bangkok's Chinatown, complete with a hubbub of vendors, lines of people waiting for the cure, and folksy signs everywhere advertising branded potions. While most of the shophouses were vacant, those adjacent to the practitioner's shop were open and selling food to the crowds that gathered.

These makeshift clinics were usually in an incongruous place, most often wherever the practitioner happened to live—be it in a row of shophouses or in some remote hamlet. Outside, vendors gathered to dispense food and drinks to the crowd. Other hangers-on appointed themselves assistants of the practitioner, handing out queue numbers and organizing appointments.

An entire cottage industry grows up around a successful clinic with branded liniments, talismans, tiny blessed statues and other palliative or symbolic items that are related to the cure. Sometimes scandals erupt when the natural remedies turn out to be deadly — especially to the liver and kidneys — but the desire to believe in these alternative therapies remains strong.

The practitioners are usually called doctors by those who believe in them. Many a foreigner has been dragged to such a doctor by a Thai girlfriend, usually with the stipulation that patients must be there by 4 a.m. They then realize this is no doctor, but a social festival where belief and hope are paramount.

The cure is usually a type of massage (massage has deep spiritual roots in Thai culture and its health beliefs) and a special balm or a natural herbal remedy. Just as in the West, things touted as "natural" or "traditional" were given special respect, even if there was little evidence for their efficacy.

Every malady is a known quantity that can be offset by those who know the proper potion. There is never any talk of uncertainty. It was easy to see how scientifically based medicine would lose out with its guarded conclusions and long-term treatments.

The ground floor of the shophouse we arrived at had been converted into a waiting room. Most there were elderly, some in wheelchairs, all hopefully waiting.

A tremor of excitement shot through the crowd as we entered. Everyone turned and raised their heads towards me and looked happy I was there — no doubt this proving that there was something to this cure if a foreigner was seeking it as well.

I had only just sat down in the waiting room when an attendant rushed over to usher me immediately to the front of the line to see the doctor. Thais usually seemed pleased to insist the foreigner go ahead, and I knew there was no stopping this offer of expedited service, especially since it reflected well on the business.

My boss and the other Thais who accompanied me headed to the next room, but the doctor himself appeared in the doorway. This prompted a titter of excitement along with an obligatory Thai *wai* from the waiting crowd. A *wai* is a sign of respect and greeting created by bringing both hands together in front of the face for a moment as if in prayer.

The doctor had a square Thai face with a hint of Indian in him and was taller and broader shouldered than the average Thai. He wore a nondescript two-piece linen outfit. I knew this was reminiscent of the various offshoot Buddhist organizations that eschewed the ordaining of monks and instead required adherents to wear uniforms every day. I was later told that this doctor belonged to no sect, but wore the custom linen suit as a sign of his holiness and novel thinking.

He looked right through me, scanning me in a way that was obviously meant to be both intimidating and convince me he was intently focused on my cure. This was part of the supposedly psychic nature of the quack practitioner. They almost always used a special sense to diagnose what was wrong.

The doctor gestured that I and those with me should enter the examination room. The room was arranged to make it look like a real doctor's office, including a high examination table with a removable paper covering and some jars of herbs on a shelf along the wall.

I sat on the table. My boss told the doctor about my tremor. Without hesitation, the doctor reached under my left collarbone and pulled on what I think was a tendon. He grasped it with tremendous force, pulling it up and away from my shoulder in a way I did not think was physically possible.

He shook me a little, chattering away to the others, saying something I did not understand, probably about the procedure. Then I began to feel numb on my left side and then very good, almost elated. Then, becoming alarmed, I said, "What's happening?" and passed out.

I convulsed a little when I regained consciousness, as I struggled to understand what was going on. Worried faces surrounded me. People were jabbering. Clearly I was not meant to pass out. This had caused extreme worry, judging by the faces studying me. The doctor was furious, speaking in intense whispers about getting me out of there.

What I think had happened was that the doctor had cut off my circulation for a moment or pinched a nerve. This might give the patient a temporary numbness or elation that could be interpreted as a cure.

Still woozy, I was grabbed underneath each arm, I do not recall by whom, and hauled out through the waiting room, my feet dragging along behind me. This caused a stir from the patients and must have been a tremendous embarrassment to the doctor.

Although they tried to get me out quickly and quietly, my dragging feet kept getting caught on chair legs in the waiting room. People leapt to their feet, gasping. When I was nearly to the door, one of my feet caught the leg of an older woman who was dozing. She jumped up from her chair, knocking it over, and let out a shriek that startled everyone. It was absolutely the most attention-getting way to leave a room.

I was placed back in the car I had arrived in. My boss and the others piled in too. I was feeling weak. Just before we drove off, the doctor stuck his head into the car and said in a worried voice and in perfectly accented English, "Don't bring him back here again." Thus I was expelled from the wisdom of the mystical East.

A few months later on a dreary rainy afternoon, I was traveling in northeastern China and toured a "renowned clinic" (they are always "renowned") outside of Changchun.

There, a Chinese expert sat across from me at an ornate table. He was only middle-aged, but had cultivated the air of a sage, with a long pointed beard and wizened eyes. He smiled and unleashed his best penetrating look while using pebbles spread on the table to diagnose what was wrong with me.

Then, in triumph, he wrote out my perceived ailments, along with a list of herbal pills and balms that I should immediately purchase from their dispensary. It was low-key and no one was pushy about selling me anything.

He was clearly hopeful that he had made the right diagnosis. I wanted to reflect his enthusiasm and confidence that he could diagnose me. I wanted to participate in this social tradition, be it a delusion or scam.

He was totally wrong in his guesses though, just like they all were, and I reluctantly left without buying anything.

AT GOVERNMENT HOUSE

I caught myself again going on about what Thailand should do to develop itself — not that there was any reason why a wanderer like myself would have any wisdom on the subject. Thais were solicitous of everything this young man said. It was seductive.

Whoever I was talking to not only passively listened to me, but encouraged me with fawning questions. No matter what I started rattling on about, everyone smiled encouragingly and appeared to agree.

The Thais had none of the visible machismo of Latin America, where people were eager to challenge my bold first-world opinions, prejudices and assumptions.

Thai culture emphasized that a gentle deference should exist between people. It was a constant awareness of the relative status of every person that informed the individual how to treat others. Age, family, riches or reputation meant being afforded unending, irrational reverence.

Thus, an opinionated foreigner found that his bold, "Say what you want and let the chips fall where they may" pronouncements would land unchallenged by the lowly and the elite alike. Behind the scenes, no doubt, their real impressions were expressed, but the foreigner rarely saw this and most probably never realized it. I certainly did not for the longest time. I was confident that my opinions mattered to this land that seemed to seek them from me.

I was encouraged, and thus encouraged myself, to talk on and on, holding forth with silly opinions, giving little speeches while all listened respectfully, becoming just like the Thai "big men" — the rich and influential — who were immune from any hint of disapproval.

Through some odd confluence of circumstances, I was sent to interview an up-and-coming politician. He was the spokesman for a new government. Fifteen years later, he would become prime minister in a contentious period of history when political rivals attempted to assassinate him during a siege of Bangkok. On that day, though, he was a young man about my own age, who I assumed would be my equal in intellect and poise. He might even need my advice.

I was driven into the government compound for the interview. Where the rest of Bangkok was typically lichen-covered shophouses, chaotic markets in the hot sun, and piles of refuse and shanties by oily railroad tracks, entering Thailand's Government House was like entering another world.

Crisply painted buildings presided over manicured lawns. Paths were immaculately maintained with not a crack or missing patch of pavement. The grounds in that small haven were planned, not shambolically added on to over decades, as in the rest of the nation.

The government spokesman's office was a stunning vintage building mixing Thai and European architectural styles. It has since been repainted frequently, but then it was colonial white with burgundy trim. Very regal.

After being shown inside, I was introduced to Abhisit Vejjajiva. He handed me his card, which was only in Thai. With his light Eton accent, he asked, "Do you think I should have it in English?"

As the interview progressed, I could not help notice that his shirt had impossibly crisp creases along the sleeves and it was brilliantly white.

I, on the other hand, as a white man moving in Bangkok at midday, had already sweated through my white shirt turned dim after multiple washings. It was devoid of any creases, as they wilted away moments after I put the shirt on.

When it came time to take his photo to accompany the article, Abhisit excused himself to put on a fresh shirt. He left to an adjacent room, where I saw dozens of freshly ironed shirts hanging in rows. He returned in a moment in both a new shirt and suit coat, perfectly tailored. I took his photo.

He was so attuned to be a spokesperson, his presentation so refined, that I was feeling more and more like what I probably really was—an underachieving slob in a foreign land.

Thinking I had escaped the judgments of my family and culture by leaving them, I was alone with my thoughts and often I congratulated myself on my own competence. I was only beginning to realize Thais rarely differentiated between a foreigner who is a scholarly academic, worthy of being lionized, and a drunken young low-class lout carrying a rumpled backpack and wearing flip flops. All were treated like kings. Thais were so kind and fearful that it drew out my own arrogance and sense of importance.

The questions I asked during the interview I have long forgotten, but I recall at the time thinking that they were the inane and uninformed questions of an outsider. The replies were so polite and politically polished that it stripped away my self-constructed sense of superiority.

I was talking with a real elite person—one ensconced in the wonder world of Government House. He was either way more competent than I was or at least had the politician's skill to make me think he was. It broke the conceit I had that Thais treated me well because it was obvious I deserved it.

I would go back to where people always agreed with me, ignored my drinking, and dropped hints which I failed to see, but the veil had been lifted. I knew then how I was deluding myself in this land. Leaving that perfect little realm of Government House and reentering the chaotic, crumbling city, I felt anxious to get back to the people who saw me as some sort of desirable hero.

NO THAIS ALLOWED

"YOU speak my language?" asked Mr. Bo.

I had absentmindedly used a few everyday Thai words, spoken out of habit, while ordering food. The Khmer driver, Mr. Bo, seated at the same table, understood them.

"Yes, those words are Khmer too," he said.

This surprised me. I knew the Thai language was close to Laotian, but I did not know it was close to Khmer, the language of Cambodians.

I was waiting to ascend to Preah Vihear Temple (or as the Thais call it, Khao Phra Viharn). It is a spectacular Angkorian-era temple that sits atop a mountain plateau that, depending on one's nationality, is an integral part of Cambodia or Thailand.

At times, the temple had been open for tourism as the only practicably accessible entry was via a grand stairway that led up the mountain on the Thai side. That access point allowed the Thais to tacitly maintain their pretense of ownership, despite an International Court of Justice ruling in 1962 that awarded the site to the Cambodians. Decades of subsequent Cambodian instability and then Thai reticence to relinquish the area had led to it becoming a no-man's land, with garrisons of soldiers on each side ready to exert their national privilege.

Eventually, the alarm was raised when the Cambodians cut their own road access from their side, bulldozing and blasting their way up the mountainside and creating a frighteningly steep road to the top. This allowed the Khmers to finally claim control of supply and tourism to the site, rendering cooperating with the Thais unnecessary. Amid further fits of sporadic shelling and political posturing on both sides, the Thais sulkily closed and mined the border, maintaining their claim that the area around Preah Vihear was part of Thailand.

From my perspective in Thailand, I knew that the Thai feeling was to consider Cambodia an alien land to be despised as a dirty and backward irritant—much like Myanmar (formerly Burma) and Laos. The roots of this Thai viewpoint are varied, but principally revolved around wars, both real and legendary, where armies had been raised and mutual conquest had resulted. This lived on in a tradition of border discrepancies, nationalistic chest thumping and political grandstanding on both sides.

I had arrived at the base of the mountain in the far north of Cambodia after a long drive over subtly rising plateaus. The new highway's concrete was already crumbling, and mini-tornadoes of discarded plastic bags swirled along the roads. Closer to Cambodian's northern border, the land rose up dramatically, with stark stone outcroppings lining the tops of mountain ridges that marked the border between Cambodia and Thailand.

"No Thais allowed" was prominently displayed on a card in plastic on the ticket desk located at the base of the mountain. Those buying tickets were first asked if they were Thai.

Only special trucks were allowed to make the climb up the road to Preah Vihear from the Cambodian side. Soon I was in one of these trucks, grinding its way up and over the stony spines of the mountain, steadily heaving over the scarily steep road. It was easy to imagine Thailand's long contentment in believing that no practical road could ever be carved into the mountain from the Cambodian side.

The truck, equipped with metal seating in the pickup bed, was piloted by Mr. Bo, a man of indeterminate age—either a young man who looked old or an old man who looked young. He exhibited both nonchalance and determination as he ground the gears all the way up the mountainside.

The final part of the drive was over a wide bulge of rock that flowed in ridges in opposition to the road. The truck struggled to maintain its direction, as if the rock's deep fissures were redirecting it off the side of the mountain. The front and back tires bounced in rhythm as we struggled on.

We finally halted at a row of souvenir stands with vendors laconically calling out their offers of t-shirts, coconut water, and beer. I tried to talk to some of them, but they only wanted to sell me things. The temple was not in sight yet, only more of the flowing rock surface that curved on and on upwards.

This was a border zone. Borders are indefinite places where one world abuts another. There is a heightened feeling of watching and being watched that creates an electric, confused, and lawless state. This sense grows as the border approaches.

Walking now, I passed a series of concrete pill boxes and gun emplacements that faced into a misty and indistinct valley, apparently towards the Thai side of the border below. Soldiers sat motionless in the heat outside of the pill boxes.

The structure that was appearing was an Angkorian temple, laid out on a long axis, familiar to anyone who has visited such places in Cambodia or northeastern Thailand. The site contained a long ceremonial staircase, twin buildings in a forecourt (sometimes referred to apocryphally in modern times as "libraries") and the central temple precepts, decorated with Hindu motifs and gods, mixed with a distinctive Angkorian style. The entire temple, like

Angkor Wat some 200 kilometers south, is assumed to be a representation of Mount Meru, home of the gods.

The complex sat above the surrounding Thai and Cambodian plains. The entire plateau sloped towards the Thai side, with outcroppings of bare rock bulging through the surface in many places. An obscuring fog hung solidly over the Thai side far below. The site was thrust too high into the sky. The glare of the sun was harsh and filled every dark place. It embodied the grandiosity of the Angkorian world perched on an incredible stone mountain. It was easy to imagine a king of old making his way to the top of this rock in the sky and saying, "From here we will look out over the lands and the people. They will look up and we will tell them that they are good."

The temple was a maze of empty rooms once filled with the items of worship and reserved as the precinct of only the initiated. Figures, carved into the walls and lintels as devotion or decoration, were now mostly indistinct, melting back into the rocks as the centuries passed. Other carvings were missing entirely—chiseled out for the illegal antiquities trade. Every window displayed an epic view of either the plains of Thailand or Cambodia.

The rear of the temple sat on the edge of steep cliffs with a 180-degree view of the plains. The lands stretched out and were quickly lost to haze—mainly forested on the Cambodian side and strictly sectioned into farms on the Thai side.

After examining one of the semi-collapsed "libraries," I noticed that Mr. Bo, the driver, was following me and apparently wanted to act as a guide. He suggested, mainly through gestures and a few English words, that I go down the temple's grand stairway towards the Thai frontier. The stairs led from the temple partway down the mountain to a cleft in the hills where a cluster of modern buildings stood. This was the original entrance to the temple from the Thai side.

The stairs were wide, but clumsy to walk on, as if they were constructed for larger-sized humans. The centuries had taken chunks out of the steps and each had to be carefully considered.

As I proceeded down, I noted the rolls of barbed wire that had been stretched across the stairs at various points in the past. Now they were bundled in tangled heaps to each side of the stairs, waiting to be pulled across again if needed. Here, at this high place, brother peoples stood face to face, still guarding the dead king's temple. Mr. Bo, who was following along, smiled broadly as if the barbed wire was incredibly amusing.

At the base of the stairs was a collection of modern-era buildings. All were starkly utilitarian and shabbily constructed when compared to the rock temple sitting on the plateau above. Some were abandoned, and those still occupied were slightly overgrown with weeds. They were apparently buildings that catered to tourists and ticket taking when the temple was only accessible from the Thai side. I looked back up and noticed that Mr. Bo had stopped midway up the stairs. I was by myself.

Outside one building, fish were laid out to dry in the sun. At another, clothes dried on a line. A woman peeked out from a doorway for a brief moment and then vanished. The air was heavy and a few massive flies whirled high above in the sunlight.

It was a short walk to the frontier. Several old trees darkened the area with their broad canopies. The practical frontier (as opposed to what Thailand claimed) was the beginning of another steep hill, which was fenced off with multiple signs warning of mines. The Cambodian side was largely cleared of foliage, but the Thai side was thickly forested with a path that led down to the border fence. The gate there was padlocked. I wondered which side possessed the key.

Behind me I sensed something and turned around to see a lone Cambodian soldier in a hammock. He warned me, through gestures, to keep back from the border gate. I approached as close to the gate as I dared and took a few photos of that impossible place between two neighbors.

Then there was a commotion. Voices were raised at the top of the stairway calling down to where I was and then back up again. It was mostly unintelligible to me, but then a voice from above called out, "Thai soldiers, Thai soldiers" in English, as if to ensure I understood what was happening.

The Cambodian soldier rolled out of his hammock and briskly shooed me back towards the modern buildings at the foot of the grand stairway. I hurried back while he and another man who emerged from the trees gathered up some rucksacks.

Suddenly the sharp sound of gunfire erupted from the Thai side. The Cambodian soldiers and their rucksacks were catching up with me and motioning for me to move along and get back to the stairs.

If I escaped without injury, this would become an adventure story tinged with danger. If I ended up dead, I would forever be recalled as reckless and unlucky.

Still unclear as to what was happening, I reached the small collection of utilitarian buildings, the drying fish and the clothes on the line, thinking unknown people with unknown motives might dash out to confront me, but I passed by without incident and then reached the bottom of the stairs. I sheltered by the stone railing that lined the stairs from bottom to top.

More spasmodic firing echoed through the hills, and it was growing closer and more insistent. It was a long way back up the stairs, so I started the inevitable climb, keeping as close to the cover of the stone banister as possible. Nearing the halfway point up, I could see clearly over to the Thai side, as several columns of soldiers marched over the hills towards the border. More popping sounds and smoke erupted from the border gate area, but I began think it did not sound like real firing after all.

A dozen more steps up and I was crouching next to a soldier and Mr. Bo, who were both sheltering there. The soldier related to me that periodically the Thais did this — set off some fireworks that simulated gunshots and then marched towards the border to test Cambodian readiness. "Still, we have to be careful," he said. He noted that allowing a foreigner — me — too near the gate might have triggered the Thais to spring one of their response drills.

More smoke rose from the border gate far below, which was now out of sight. I imagined the Thai military men arriving to check the gate and affirm their right to be there.

This readiness drill did not evoke much martial response from the Cambodian side. Only a handful of soldiers in various states of repose had been stationed near the border. No vehicles or visible weapons other than those near the pill boxes way back by the souvenir stands were visible.

On the Thai side in the distance I could see a modern and elaborate building on the next big hill over the border. A Thai flag stood prominently near the building. This was the flagpole that once was located proudly at Preah Vihear. Instead of lowering the flag when they vacated the site, the Thais moved the flagpole and flag intact to its present location to demonstrate their defiance.

The Thai building was covered with an array of antennas — the kind that indicate serious official business. In front was a parking lot where both military vehicles and cars were parked. A line of soldiers was marching towards the border gate in the foreground. Neat and professional barbed wire fences could be seen, as well as orderly paths and paved roads. It was very much in the style of governmental and military buildings and their manicured grounds in Thailand. These were no sleepy, moldering third world buildings as per Western stereotype. In Thai officialdom, everything was state-of-the-art with no expense spared.

Eventually, the general state of alarm simply ceased. The Cambodian soldiers sat back down in bits of shade, and the handful of tourists, mostly Chinese, resumed wandering about in the sun.

The Cambodian soldiers I met smiled as if the events of the day were amusing. It could have been a smile in the Thai-style — indicating unease and embarrassment, but in that place and in that confusion, it was hard to make a judgment. The location was too unusual, the border soldiers too tense.

One soldier was wearing a more formal uniform — complete with elaborate insignia — standing under one of the few trees on the plateau. He stood beside a monocular on a tripod aimed at the Thai side.

Indicating in pantomime that I wished to take a look, I approached the monocular. The soldier ignored me and was standing a couple feet from the scope, so I presumptuously crept nearer, watching to see if he would object if I looked through it. He regarded me with apparent boredom, but also a tiny bit of attention, as if he was noticing a beetle crawling along.

I peered into the scope and saw the Thai side through shimmering heat. The Cambodian soldier had the scope trained on the modern Thai military building, which appeared to be a small office building or visitors' center surrounded by officious military personnel and equipment. Expensive cars and brand new troop vehicles came and left the parking lot, as they do throughout Thailand. All Thais drive or desperately wish to.

Then I realized that right in the middle of it was a spotter with a scope on the Thai side. He was looking back at me with military professionalism. Something about his posture made me realize he was intensely engaged in figuring out why I was looking back at him.

I raised my hand and waved. There was no response.

I waved again and nothing changed. I finally pulled my eye away from the scope. The Thai side and its spotter receded back into the never-ending hills that we each stood upon.

The Khmer soldier still regarded me without expression. I thanked him. Perhaps he made a slight acknowledgment, a softening of his face for the briefest of moments. Perhaps not. It was hard to tell.

The sun was too close to that high place and the ultraviolet light and glare reflected in every direction as it hit the rock outcroppings across the plateau. I knew the types of country boys who ended up in the Thai military by virtue of their lack of money or influence to exempt themselves from the draft. I had been in Phnom Penh when soldiers raided a disco and carted off young men — dragooned into a hungry military. I assumed the Cambodian side was also filled with lowly young men forced to serve, called to this high and bright place, as were the Thais.

It was alien — this temple that reflected the splendor and rights of kings when Angkor prospered. In its bold and exposed location, so remote, it was heavily guarded by modern men who hardly seemed to have any connection to the mysterious kingdoms of long ago.

As I passed the souvenir stands again on the way back to the truck, I was thinking that I was probably sunburned. Mr. Bo tried to explain something to me, but it was hard to understand his meaning. The truck heaved down the hill, roaring and inching along in turn. Dust wafted through the truck, no doubt trod upon by those a millennium before.

CLOUDS

"Is that yours?" she said.

I was looking at a photo I took years before I met her. It was of an old-style Chinese hotel lobby in Taipei. It had high ceilings and a cot by the check-in desk where the owner slept so that he might man the front desk around the clock. A moon-faced child was in the foreground of the photo, toddling towards the camera.

The genderless child had the blank look of the empty young, eyes open, but no thought. It could have been a lost child, wandering and missing someone. The photo was faded and the colors in the interior of the small, enclosed lobby were muted and brown. It looked as if it could have been taken 50 years ago.

My wife was looking over my shoulder at the photo. "Is that yours?" she repeated.

It was a surprising question. I saw that she was holding out the possibility that I was wistfully looking at a photo of a long-lost child of mine, carelessly conceived and abandoned long ago.

I told her no. I felt sorry that I seemed like a person who would have hidden such a secret — that I would have fathered a child with another, but not with her. We never would have a child together, but on that day, I did not know that, and I just told her, "No, it is not my child."

I had married out of my race, out of my nationality, in a place where men were expected to be careless. Selfishness was considered as much a part of manliness as unfounded pride.

The photo was from one of many times I had visited Taipei. I had traveled there to source computer parts for a company in Thailand. Computers in Thailand were taxed as a luxury item — considered a thing that a normal person did not need and thus were a wonton extravagance that sent precious Thai currency overseas.

The calculation was that importing parts and then assembling the computers in Thailand made more sense than buying the computer as an assembled piece from overseas and attracting the luxury tax.

I spent many days in a warren of basements in a computer components market in Taipei, shoulder to shoulder with local nerds bidding on baskets of parts that would later be soldered onto boards to create computers for the rich to enjoy in their luxury homes in sunny Thailand.

The light in Taipei, however, was perpetually dull, as if the region were underground. A low blanket of overcast sky stretched out from the surrounding mountains and pressed down on the city, casting it in a continual twilight. It was always cold and rainy. The city was both industrious and subdued in its blandness. It was the quintessence of the Asian Tiger city — concrete boxes and shophouses, utilitarian high rises — all stretching out in uniform and chaotic waves into endless sprawl.

Cars were the symbol of the affluence of the age and new luxury autos littered the roads. Two or three layers of double parking reduced side streets to a trickle of incomprehensible traffic. I did not have a car in Asia and could never hope to have one, as the taxes were several hundred percent of the car's value, thus making the most basic of cars cost as much as a Mercedes back in the West. Still, more and more cars were bought every day. There was money out here. People had it. I had made my choice. This was where I lived.

One day I took the bus to the outskirts of town to go to the National Palace Museum. The Kuomintang had taken as much Chinese art and artifacts with them as they could when they repaired to Taiwan in 1949, as if the possession of these items conferred legitimacy on the exiled state. They took so much that, at any one time, reportedly only one percent of the treasures could be displayed.

The oracle bones were on display at the museum then. Millennia old, they were used for divination and held examples of the earliest Chinese writing. Questions were scratched on the bones and then they were cast into the fire. Will I be prosperous? Will I sire children? By some method long forgotten, the way the heat of the fire broke the bones answered the questions.

The Chinese characters scratched on to the bones were proto-forms of Chinese writing and some of the proper names were no longer translatable, as the unique characters could not be linked to sounds. The answers to the entreaties written on the bones must have long been answered, but the questions themselves remained etched into the bones. I was thankful that I happened to be there to see them.

Back in town, it was liberating to walk where no one knew me or noticed me. I moved along, from nondescript street to street, my mind clear of past or future. The shop signs were mainly indecipherable and thus I did not have to read any words in my mind as I walked by. What went on inside those buildings? Possibly nothing.

Then there was the gaming district. It was mainly a business-to-business zone where the latest technologies were on display. One section had shops with large-screen console games placed on the sidewalks in front.

A thrilling new fighting game was on display. Figures in electric colors leapt at each other, punching and colliding. I had never before seen a video game as elaborate and detailed. It was stunning. A crowd surrounded the large screen, all wrapped in brown and grey coats, steeled against the cold winds, transfixed by the figures on the screen. The characters, their movements, and the backgrounds were so bright and lifelike that I wanted to stand and watch forever.

That night, like a tourist, I ate at the Hard Rock Cafe in the heart of the city. I sat alone under a photo of Pete Townsend on the wall behind me, his hand bloody, looking bored. There must have been things happening in the layers of buildings where lives were lived just like mine, but I did not know them and they did not know me.

Then I made an effort to go to the red-light district. It was an area of dark, but oddly clean and orderly alleys. I had read the warnings about the place such as fistfights erupting when passersby were grabbed and dragged into a dingy bar for a drink, along with other warnings of scams and horrors. These tales could have been made up by do-gooders to prevent people from visiting the area. No one grabbed me and I witnessed no horrors. I did not see much or dare to go inside. I just glided through unnoticed.

On the way back to my hotel, I stopped at a convenience store. These shops all had large jars holding boiled eggs doused in brown soy sauce. I watched intently as the middle-aged proprietor robotically dipped a ladle deep into the still, brown liquid to fish out a petrified boiled egg in soy sauce. I loved eating those eggs.

The streets were empty. The sky was still vague, in uniform shadow, illuminated by street lights.

Then I was back in my dark hotel room looking at the ceiling. I did not want to move and just let my mind drift.

I do not recall when, but at some point I took a photo in the hotel lobby with the child toddling towards the camera.

At the airport, as I was leaving on yet another plane, people walked back and forth or stood in lines that never really ended. People were arriving and people were leaving.

That was not my child. Nothing ever happens.

A FOREST DARK

THE few times I saw myself in the mirror—really saw myself—I was startled by the vacancy in my eyes. Most days, though, I could only perceive the day ahead, being late, and being annoyed at the petty grievances of rushing from one place to another.

Standing at the mirror in the morning, getting ready for work, I heard the *tokays* calling, "To-kay, to-kay!" These calls were interspersed with the panicky crowing of roosters that also existed in the nooks of the city. The *tokays* were giant geckos as rare to see as they were common to hear in those early days. In the present day, something about the city—its density, its dust, its unrelenting cement—seems to have finally quieted them, but back then they were a bracing surprise every time I heard them. I imagined they challenged me each morning with their croaks.

I was originally intoxicated with traveling during my first years in Asia, boldly following news of any possible adventure and moving ever outward. I travelled along the border with Myanmar where rebel groups held and lost territory from month to month, hiked to the furthest ruins I could find in Cambodia, and followed watercourses over what I imagined must surely be uncharted waterfalls in Vietnam. Ever outward. "To-kay, to-kay!" the lizards called.

When I heard about a hike across the narrowest part of Thailand to the Myanmar border, I naturally wanted to go along. It was on the Kra Isthmus, near the site of multiple attempts to create a canal to cross the Gulf of Siam to the Andaman Sea. The trek was arranged by a friend who gathered orchids and sold them at markets. As I learned later, that was a highly illegal activity. Still, this friend was also a cheerful police officer — police usually known as overseers of local criminal activity.

To get to the hiking point, I first had to take a *songthaew*. This was typically an old pickup truck lined with benches in the bed, or, in my case, a late-model American sedan. The farther south one went in Thailand, the more large cars were used for intra-provincial transport.

I boarded the empty car and expected a comfortable ride to the trailhead, but then I realized it would not leave until it was fully packed with passengers and cargo. Over the next 45 minutes it did fill up completely with people and bundles, until we were all wedged in, clown-car fashion.

I was dropped off at a sandy path. I traversed the last kilometers on the back of a motorcycle through four-meter-high stands of palm-like weeds. They smelled so vaguely fragrant that I wanted to keep going forever to be able to finally capture the full scent. Once I made it through, I realized that the weeds were sharp and had left cuts on my arms.

At the trailhead, I joined a group of eight grim-looking local people, along with the orchid collector. Various bundles and song birds in a cage were waiting to be carried to some remote location by those in the group. I received a few curious looks, but I put on my mild innocuous smile and was soon ignored again. The bundles were hoisted up and we began.

The trail was initially faint and it appeared that we were cutting directly through the jungle. Eventually, a little path was born, perhaps made by wildlife, with bushes and trees on either side reaching in across the trail. The sun found places to drop into the canopy, mostly in dappled light, but sometimes a refreshing clear shaft of light reached to the ground.

We climbed up and over a series of waterfalls, most of the time crawling on our hands and knees for balance. The levels of the falls were created by a series of crude cement dams already crumbling apart, and I was disappointed when I realized they were man-made. The orchid collector stopped to clip small sprigs of plants and pull off little bundles of stems from the trees. I was motioned to keep quiet and move quickly. Only later did I realize that we had moved clandestinely through a national park.

We trekked on, following a watercourse increasingly filled with life — wriggling things, insects, fishes, floating mosses, and decay.

Some blood had to be given up to the mosquitoes and other unseen things. Any time I stepped off the trail, I walked into massive webs and disturbed exotic spiders. I imagined the webs warned humans from straying into dangerous territory.

The forest was made of odd angles of twisted tree limbs. Great boulders were cleaved in strange places, creating impressive and incomplete arrowheads, their edges sharp in the sunlight.

I fell into a brisk pace, my body marching in martial motion alongside the locals who merely sauntered along the trail, making the same or better time than I did. This life was made for walking.

The waters dwindled away, and at some point which I did not notice, vanished entirely. Then I walked in the hot dry of the jungle and the humidity that could slake no thirst.

A Burmese man tried to explain to me in garbled English that it was easy to step on and be bitten by a snake. If that happened, one would likely die, as it would be impossible to get back to help in time. I was already aware of this and wore jeans and heavy shoes, but noted that every other person (including the man warning me) was in shorts and flip flops.

With a sad nod of his head, he said that the land was not fertile. I found I was a bit dizzy as I forced myself on.

Particularly in Thailand's climate, it was easy to see what nature really was to a human — a foe to be fought and tamed. It was not a natural landscape for people to thrive in. The weather was brutally hot and wet and the bugs were unrelenting. I wondered how past generations had the energy to do it. It was an immediately consuming place — living innards that every creature sank into to be recycled.

I wondered if the cement box cities that sprang forth when nations first developed were a response to this — to stifle and keep out the uncomfortable natural world that made humans suffer so much.

My own toil that day took me away from things I could not really name at the time. I kept going from place to place without stopping. It was too much thinking over too long a time. With each new year came seeing the world and its dangers and its possibilities in an increasingly realistic light. I was tired of working and even of adventuring. I was tired of considering it all. I knew I could not go back to my home country to live, eating out at fast food restaurants, talking about cleaning gutters, and buying everything on credit. I thought I was smarter than everyone else for escaping from the West. It was my badge of honor. It was not depression or any other trendy way to think. It was just being tired and then running away, but still being tired when I got there.

Blazing noontime passed and I was drenched with sweat, as if a bucket of water had been dumped over my head. Then there was the elation and abandon of being soaked, like falling into a pool fully clothed, but laughing and splashing in the water. It was not water, of course, but my own salty sweat. It was like blood coming out of every pore — cooling blood, my own internal chemicals, exuding endlessly.

I felt I was nearing some inevitable change. It was to be a new phase where I had to be a man and settle down. It was not anything most people resisted. On the contrary, others rushed to pair off, not use a condom and get locked into the proper life that everyone is supposed to want. The children, the divorces, and the necessity to lose five days a week to work were no barrier. In fact, those who resisted this life were accused of being juvenile or gay.

I was resisting arrival at this new place. These thoughts wore on me, and escaping to the other side of the world had not helped after all. Maybe something was wrong with me. I could only go on like this for so long. I was not good enough and I was not sure I ever could be. Now I was going as far west as possible before hitting the closed border of Myanmar. There would be no further to go.

The peak of late afternoon came and heat built up in the jungle, even under the canopy. This was long before the days when everyone carried bottles of water as a matter of habit and I never thought to bring any extra supply. I would just drink water when I had the chance, so I was likely dehydrated.

One of the men trekking with us explained that he was traveling to a village across the border in Myanmar. He had three children by now, as his wife was pregnant when he left. "New baby!" he said brightly.

He worked on a Thai fishing vessel, as so many Myanmar migrants did and was away from home for a year at a time. On his back he was awkwardly carrying a TV wrapped in plastic and a Super Famicom video game system in a heavily taped box. He was lovingly bringing back these treasures to his family, who had no idea he was returning. I was amazed he would do this. He had a wrinkled, almost pained smile of lifelong resignation from working under difficult conditions in a foreign land on the harsh sea for his family.

We entered a cool lowland and the group went silent and stopped. A titter of excitement moved through the hikers. Far down the hill to the left of us, something was moving. I felt the excitement of the moment even before I saw anything. At first I was barely able to glimpse it through the foliage and distance, but then I clearly saw a large thing emerge from the mud it was wallowing in.

It was shiny black with a low-slung head and a pig-like body, and it had a distinct erect unicorn-like horn. Maybe it was some sort of forest buffalo or cattle—that was the obvious guess, but it really looked like a little rhinoceros — otherwise long extinct in the region. Then, in an instant, it jumped up from the mud and was forever gone, vanishing into the forest leaves. The group debated what it was as we continued on, but eventually fell silent again.

At the beginning of a new adventure there was no thought of the past or future. There was only the open and unknown of the immediate voyage. It was a bracing forgetting that lasted until about the middle of the journey, then the thoughts of having to go back to work — the uncertain future and the unsatisfactory present — returned. I sensed this was the mid-point of my trip.

I started to anticipate the end of the hike and having to wait for the *songthaew* to take me back from where I had come. I thought of what I had to do the next week and how I would pick up my little briefcase and walk through the city in my rumpled white shirt to work again.

The heat pressed in. We were heading west, pushing against the heavy hot air. I was walking slower and slower, dragging myself to the destination. Stopping for even a second caused a mass of biting insects to descend upon me. Finally, the sun was blocked by a looming black mountain, providing some shade. I was far, far from anything, I proudly thought, and still a few hours from my destination at the Myanmar border.

The cicadas then started their chirping, triggered by the gathering shade. They shrieked from every tree. This was a signal for the mosquitoes too. They began buzzing in my ears and nose.

I wandered off the trail to relieve myself, stumbling and crashing through the underbrush awkwardly. I stepped on a tree root which rose up, wavered in the air for a moment and then bit me on the thigh, right through my pants. It was more like a punch than a bite, like being violently hit with the end of a long pole. It made me stagger back.

The snake was still attached, its mouth wiggling on my leg. Suddenly my wits were about me and I carefully pulled it up and off my leg and flung it away, nearly getting bitten again as I threw it.

I do not know if the others had been watching me as I went off the trail or if I shouted and did not know it, but the group was immediately around me. In the ensuing ruckus, I was laid down back on the trail, with the other hikers regarding me and jabbering in obviously worried tones.

Knowing little of the language then, I imagined they were saying something like, "This would only happen to the clumsy foreigner we brought along" or "We're going to get blamed for this."

I did not feel any pain, but I thought I felt warmth in the region of the bite, as if a blanket was beginning to grip my leg. For a moment in the tumult after I was bitten, I could have gone either way — panicky or deathly calm. I just decided to be calm. Something had already happened.

The concerned group led me away from the trail at a ninety-degree angle, quickly up and down over hills and across gullies, with vines smashing into my face the entire way. The hike was ruined, I guess, but I just went on quietly, feeling the bite and the growing ache in my leg, and pain extending up into my torso.

I wondered if I should be worried. Thinking this surprised me. I was supposed to panic, but did not. I felt it inside me. It had happened. I would just feel calmer and calmer as the pain increased I thought. Nothing more to be concerned about. The things I was supposed to do could no longer vex me. The damnable hows and whys of the necessities of living — paying the rent, renewing my visa, my next paycheck — would no longer be priorities. I would not have to be a man or anything else. I had done the last of everything. It had just stopped on this trail with no further consequences. It was no longer my problem. All things lifted from my mind and this strangely elated me. I was carefree at last, even as my leg began to feel swollen.

I had never gotten up the courage to try to kill myself before — I had just pondered it until I felt what a relief it would be. It was always there as an option, but only as long as I was alive. It would be a preposterous thing to actually do. After dying I would be seen as some sort of loser by the very people I was trying but unable to impress in life. Still I could not resist thinking how it would be to finally quiet the mind — nothing to consider or worry about any longer. The actual doing of the thing was the real concern, so gigantic in consequence that I could not bear to focus on the practical steps necessary to accomplish it.

Now the mechanics of death were taken care of. It was so much better than a cancer diagnosis and its long drawn-out torture that cheated one of the joys of the weight of life being lifted.

Then it was completely dark. We were in a clearing. The moon was lighting the bluish star-speckled sky. I lay in my underwear on the cool hard mud, the hikers having pulled off my pants to examine the wound. I was dizzy and beginning to feel sick. I watched a large black ant crawl up my leg to investigate the puncture wounds. I thought I felt my leg pulse.

"This is perfect. Just keep my mind light." I made sure not to think of family or lost loves or any deep thing, just of the relief from the obligations I put upon myself. Inevitability. I relaxed, and the heat and sweat of the forest held me close.

I closed my eyes, just to rest. I told myself, "This is perfect." The novelty of the world was wearing out. It cannot last.

I remember myself on the trail and the way I accepted what had happened. I was there, still in my body and completely convinced I was in reality, but I was also in another place, welcomed by several people, and I did not question them. I knew what was happening. I was in a vivid perfect place.

This was something different, because I did not care for anything or any person. It was a new kind of living, entirely cut off from my physical self and its worries back in the jungle.

I was me, but everything I thought was me was no longer there. It no longer clawed at me. I did not care about any person, relative, or love — and I knew with certainty that one day they would realize what they really were too. I was not worried. I did not yearn for another. I cared for no slight. It was all equal, and to know this, I only had to lose my flesh. This was me all along, but I did not know it before. It was the freshest, most elated state I had ever experienced, clarified by the reptile's poison pouring through me.

A person led me across a green plaza. It was no longer a dream, but real. This is where I would be now, I was told.

I marveled that the experiences I had endured in the flesh — the worries, the yearning, the agitation — were now completely gone. I knew of them, but could no longer grasp them. I thought to myself, "This is incredible. This is what it is like to be the real me."

I awoke, almost with a start, as a sweaty doctor was poking at my wound with some instrument. Others moved about as if they had just been busily attending to my care. I was on a metal table and realized I had awoken because one of my shoulder blades was pushing uncomfortably against the hard surface. The doctor snapped his fingers to rouse me. "You, you," he said.

"I'm ok," I replied, and tried to look like I was indeed alert to show I was now alive.

I had been sent back. I was quietly angry at first, both that I was alive and that I had dared to wish to die in the first place. Another part of my mind was clearing and I recalled being half-carried, half-dragged from my repose on the hard earth to a pickup truck. We must have been near a road or nearly at our destination when I was bitten. I did not know how much time had passed.

Apparently the bite had missed a huge artery in my leg, so that had given me some time, and I had received many vials of anti-venom which was a miracle cure. I stayed in the clinic overnight, watched over by a team of nurses.

The next morning I caught myself in a mirror. My eyes were full of intensity and my hair was tousled and standing on end as if I had just awakened.

"It would have been perfect," I thought, but now it was forever too late. On the forest floor, then and there, I could have died happily, I think. I could have decided, with such peace, to just go — through the jungle and on to a new place. I still remember how I felt, but I know I could not feel that way again. I was back in the world and could remember everything there was to do. It came rushing back and I was in the heat and lurching buses and Buddhist temples. This was what was next and I could do it.

Whether my vision was a glimpse of truth or a dying brain offering up an ego-soothing last memory, I did not know. Whatever it was, it did make me less fearful. There was a peace I could not really feel yet, but it was out there. I hope I have that dream again, whatever it was, when the time finally comes someday.

I was sick to my stomach on the bus back to Bangkok and would feel achy all over for several more days. After arriving at the main bus station at the west of town, I had 18 baht left. The rest of my money had been spent on my medical treatment.

What was left was enough for a city bus ticket to take me the rest of the way into town or I could buy a Coca-Cola and walk back. Thai shops served Coke with a straw in a little baggie full of ice. I felt sick and achy and was concerned about walking all the way back in my state, but I wanted a Coke. Finally I decided to spend what I had on something to drink.

The pitched roofs loomed as I walked back into Bangkok. It was late and bright and I could not see the details, only sharp outlines. I was no longer afraid I might be too weak to go on. The buses rumbled by, rattling apart and trailing clouds of tumbling black dust. I keep moving my feet, as it all remained there, sharp against the sky.

EMBASSY DAYS

I had not quite stumbled across why I might be a good hire, but when I later began hiring people myself, I discovered the reason. I expected to interview the stereotypical traveler of Lonely Planet lore — earnest, willing to work hard, and looking for an interesting adventure in a foreign land.

More often, I interviewed an alcoholic derelict who would never have been tolerated in the businesses of his home country. Those reeking of drink when arriving at a job interview emphasized the fact by preemptively declaring that they were only wearing a lot of cologne. Sometimes it would be a sensitive nerd who could not get a girlfriend in his homeland and would rail on about the fat-butted feminists that he felt dogged him. Sometimes it was an older, odd-ball libertarian, unable to accept the incongruities of the world. Sometimes they were just eccentric — a square peg that would not fit into their own society's round hole.

These people found relief and liberation in the Thai universe. Their neuroses festered in new and weird directions, but Thai employers and girlfriends saw nothing unusual about their quirks — they were just how Westerners were known to be.

My own advantages as a hire were that I did not come to an interview smelling of whisky, I did not reek of sweat, and I was not too grizzled looking. Also, although I probably had many weird opinions, I possessed the good sense not to immediately state them all and demand that others concur. I just had to pretend I was normal, and that made me stand out from the peculiar foreigners who tended to gravitate towards Thailand.

It was the odd truth for the job-hunting foreigner in Bangkok that the interviewer did all the talking. This was likely due to the type of ambitious, risk-taking, slightly crazy person who dared to open a business. The young men from the West who washed up on Thai shores with dreams to file the paperwork and finagle the money required to start a company were a special breed. Any foreign-registered business or those with many foreign shareholders were singled out for official scrutiny. Raising your head and doing things the legal way meant alerting the authorities that you were a rich foreigner who deserved to be fined by officialdom.

So I was interviewed for a job. The boss, who I will call Mr. Jones, talked and talked. The men who ran these Bangkok businesses were more interested in making sure potential hires were impressed by their achievements and knowledge rather than asking questions of those they interviewed. He explained to me that his company compiled economic and political reports for clients who were interested in such information.

Mr. Jones was like they all were — pasty white, lean, and garrulous. He spoke in generalizations. "We are the glue that holds the world together. The more information the better," he explained, but I was pretty sure he did not know what he was talking about. Mountains of data only obscured the world. Most of my time as an analyst was pointing at one or two sentences in a report and saying, "That's it" — that is the crux of it — that was what was going to happen next.

So I was hired by Mr. Jones with a handshake and began work in the strange world of predicting the future.

Mr. Jones was likable, and at his best selling his business to clients, but detached from the logistics of running his company. Like many expat business owners, he was rarely in the office. The day-to-day operations were chaotic and the accounting was atrocious.

At the start of each week, I read the intelligence guidance that listed what the U.S. was interested in. Are the Muslims taking over? Are there any moves to restrict cigarette sales? Who is selling knock-off copies of drugs? Are there any border disputes that could go violent? All things the twentieth century's Roman Empire was interested in.

No one cared that much about conflict or fighting *within* Thailand — unless Muslims were involved and unless the supply chain (for American factories exporting from Thailand) might be disrupted.

During one period of political unrest in Bangkok, I was surprised to realize that reports of the discord were of little interest to the embassies — after all, it was not a border dispute and thus could be of little consequence. However, U.S. multinationals were frantically trying to determine from the embassy the odds that shipping might be disrupted — meaning that their goods made in Thailand might not make it back to U.S. consumers. Americans assume that their government does, and perhaps should, intervene in the internal affairs of other countries, but it was amusing to find out that this intervention was most often to secure supply chains for big U.S. companies that outsource jobs to overseas factories.

I hung the supposed Anand Panyarachun quote, "Never underestimate the darkness in Thailand" over my desk. Thailand was so smiling, so welcoming, so admirably predictable, that it was easy to lose sight of how dangerous things could suddenly become. The desire for brutality to solve problems was due to the lack of strong courts, as well as corrupt rural authorities eager to cooperate with wrongdoers. This meant that violence and liquidation were seen as commonsense remedies.

I was first assigned to write up briefs of political parties to compare their policies. This was on the assumption that political parties everywhere must be about issues, but none of the Thai political parties had policies like U.S. political parties — nor could they be said to be right or left. They were merely associations of influential men and women who bound themselves together for the benefit of their families or companies, without regard for anything except the desire to be part of a sitting government.

This reality did not sit well with those reading the reports. They insisted that political parties must be left or right. They must be conservative or liberal, along Western lines.

I consulted with a few Western academic experts who could recount, as if by rote, what was happening in the nation's politics and history, but even they had little interest in knowing the mind of the Thai and *why* it was happening. Most assumed things did not happen the way a Westerner thought they should because Thailand was "still developing," and that the highest reaches of government was unluckily filled with an inordinate number of sociopaths.

Neighboring Vietnam had been a painful lesson for the Americans. For decades afterwards, it damaged the American's belief that they knew what they were doing. It challenged the assumption that hard work and sustained effort could solve any problem. Americans thought they were always the good guys, but Vietnam taught them that, not only could the good guys lose, but that the Americans might not be the good guys in the first place.

Years passed since the unfortunate incongruities of Vietnam. In the diplomatic corps, at least from my anecdotal perspective, there was no longer any sense that the American man was any different or came from any motivational background different from that of any other person on Earth.

The end of the Cold War heightened this. It created a feeling in the U.S. about the inevitability of history every bit as fervent as when communists thought all human history was a march towards communism. The collapse of the Soviet empire led to a certainty in the U.S. that history was an inexorable march towards capitalism, democracy, and international harmony.

These beliefs are hard to talk people out of. I quickly developed an appreciation of the motivations of actions in the "Thai world" (as I liked to call it). For instance, Westerners felt no particular unease with protest. After all, it was an admirable thing, part of one's freedom of expression.

When following Thai events, it was easy to see that protest was seen differently. Protest was an angry last resort, thought of as a shame on society, since it demonstrated that people could not work together and thus had to protest. This shattered the idyllic and cooperative state that the land was supposed to have. This meant that protesters were supposed to be irrational, even violent, to shame those who forced them to protest in the first place.

Beyond this, no Thai I spoke to ever considered the validity of any protest, as they thought the protesters were tarred by being part of someone else's agenda. It was indeed clear that political figures were often behind protests for their own ends at certain times, paying off and utilizing the poor or otherwise dispossessed.

The Thai academics I conferred with were content to live in a world where there were no real grievances — protest was only something to be disparaged. It was never real. The entreaties of the poor were to be disregarded because some third party might be behind a protest and benefit from it.

Whether the protesters were people pushed too far by events beyond their control or paid to protest, it was said that they were giving up their lives by protesting, since protest was a societal shame and could cause a violent counterreaction.

Even this had a follow-on — that those organizing protests were seeking a brutal reprisal against the protesters to be able to demand that those in power step down to show contrition for the violent situation that their policies created by sparking a violent protest in the first place.

That was just one example of how different things were in Thailand and how it challenged my assumptions as a Westerner. I wondered how many other countries the U.S. was interpreting wrongly.

These differing definitions extended to other aspects of behavior in the Thai political world and obviously had great ramifications for how events were interpreted, and, most importantly, predicted.

Using some overall principles of how and why things happen that I had developed (or rediscovered, since others must have known this in the past), I started following certain dates and locations to try to predict what events might transpire.

I found these predictions coming together as I wrote up an analysis. By describing the events and their underpinnings, this automatically pointed to the next event, as long as the motivators in the Thai system could be accepted on their own terms.

The embassy types still thought that the American's view of common sense and motivations was universal. Thinking this is even a part of the American's egalitarianism — contending all people are equal and thus the same in any culture. When Thais did things differently than expected, the embassy types chalked it up to them being ridiculous, uneducated, or corrupt. It was lucky there was no jungle war going on in Thailand, because the Americans would surely have lost it.

The U.S. embassy's focus, outside of securing supply lines for multinationals, was law enforcement. At any time, two FBI agents were stationed in Bangkok (provided extra compensation as Bangkok was then still a "hardship posting") to oversee the continual stream of fugitives fleeing to the country.

Thailand was a valuable honey trap. Its presumed chaotic remoteness attracted the scum of America and Europe, but they were quickly caught (at least in those days) and sent back — usually with as little fanfare as Thai authorities could manage.

As Thailand was a relatively unimportant country that cooperated with every foreign security force and studiously desired to be on no side — at least overtly — there was little desire to focus too much attention on the country. It had no firm stance and wanted to be friends with all. It was always a pliable ally and its government was easily bent to the will of overseas entreaties.

There was much the embassies did not know and did not care to know. Anything out of the ordinary could be assigned to the illogic of the Thai — the proof of which was seemingly apparent in the city everywhere.

At times I attended cocktail parties in high rises with plush carpeted floors and plenty of potbellied Americans in their requisite and uniform blue suits. At once it was as far from Thailand as one could possibly be, as well as generic — there was no hint of what country the gathering was being held in. The diplomats were interested in terrorism, increasingly hysterical over Muslims, and focused on what was going on politically in the U.S. If I started to talk about Thai politics, eyes glazed over and people would drift away.

Intelligence and insight about a country was still thought to come from having drinks with a highborn connected person who was thrilled at the honor of being asked to drink with foreign diplomats. The Americans assumed that since they were talking to an elite person, they would get the real story of what was going on. However, in any culture, the higher the person in rank or power, the less they really know what is going on. With elevation comes isolation. Those in high positions who believed they knew what was going on were only deluded.

What few Americans knew was that to get Thais to talk truthfully, one had to pretend to have no opinion. Opinionated foreigners never heard the truth in Thailand — neither did anyone who asked many questions. Those things only made the Thais hide their true opinion in public, or, even worse, made them mindlessly parrot the presumed opinions that foreigners around them expressed.

The Thai needed stillness. In the presence of an admiring listener and an absence of conflicting opinions, one had just to listen and a Thai would tell everything they knew. There were no secrets in Thailand, just bad listeners.

For years I wondered what the embassy types did with their cocktail party banter and if it was really considered important intelligence. Only many years later, when the Wikileaks release of U.S. cables occurred, was it clear that the embassy types did scramble to write up every detail of their conversations with the highborns as important information that revealed something about Thailand. I am certain the Thais at those parties were shocked that their gossip was treated with such gravity by the Americans.

The upshot of Wikileaks is that embassy types will no longer be provided with cocktail party musings from top Thais. Throughout the world, people will think twice before gossiping to American officials again.

A few clients were happy to receive a briefing and accept the realities of the Thai world. This was a refreshing change from skeptics who needed exhaustive explanations of why Thai events did not transpire in the exact same way an American expected.

It was not easy. Embassy people in particular were focused on their own internal goals. There did not seem to be much desire for real knowledge about the country and it motivators. This was coupled with the idea that "We already subscribe to the newspapers" and thus we know what is going on.

I began to see the patterns of thought. For instance, America's foreign enemies had to be described in a certain way. They were always in poor health, corrupt, about to fall from power any day, and only cared about money. Years later, I was not surprised when the first reports about Osama bin Laden emphasized how unhealthy he was (supposedly kidney ailments), as if it validated how America's enemies were physically decaying. It said more about the observer than the observed.

Belgium and the Netherlands both were interested in the company's analysis and took me to lunch several times, but they did not accept that other cultures had a version of common sense different than their own. For example, the Thai police gave the embassies some preposterous story about the culprits of a bombing and the embassy people were adamant that this was the true story. The real story was only in the Thai-language press, not accessible to the insular embassy people. In the Thai-language press, the police exonerated the culprits, and the real, politically associated cause of the blast was discussed at length. Faced with this, the Belgium Embassy official sniffed, "We are only stationed here for two years, so it doesn't matter."

This was the joy of Thailand too. It was impenetrable. I think the Thais liked it that way. Not taught to put themselves in another's shoes, there is simply too much of a gulf to explain the whys of their world to the insistent, opinionated, haughty foreigner.

The foreigner in Thailand could remain isolated with their opinions evolving, over time, into contempt, never having to touch the muck and sadness of the Thais. They could barely understand the passivity of the office worker who rides to work two hours a day on a lurching bus in the rain and never breathes a word of complaint. The blank faces of the passengers and those waiting by the road do not betray a hint of agitation or impatience. Using American tropes of understanding, it can never be understood why endless cycles of elected governments do not confront corrupt practices or enforce the law.

I was sometimes accused of working for the CIA. Maybe I did; I was not sure. I worked for a company that worked for a company that probably was subcontracted to various businesses and agencies. Apparently, such chains of companies were set up to ensure that there could be no congressional oversight to determine whether information was obtained through threats or bribes — thought to be the only way to get real intelligence, but, ironically, the least likely way of obtaining correct information.

I smugly went about this work for a good long while, boldly predicting this and that. Eventually, I correctly predicted the location of a bombing, and, shortly afterwards, an attack. No one congratulated me. Instead, I was accused of having some inside links to "bandits" or that I even helped stage the events to make myself look good.

The world was full of jobs where one is supposed to go the extra mile to do a good job. The reward is usually just a meager salary, but in this case, I was accused of being a terrorist and risked losing everything.

It taught me that prescience is best applied to making money on stock trades and to keep my analysis to myself. It is too dangerous to tell the future out loud.

A SKETCH OF PENANG

AT each stop, radiant young girls boarded the bus, some carrying straw cages containing chickens that clucked in short bursts. The girls wore full-bodied robes in muted colors with only their faces fetchingly exposed. More and more people got on, lobbing bulky parcels into the open windows of the bus before boarding through the door at the front. The passengers chatted together amiably in yet another language I did not understand, as rain-scented air flooded in through the open windows.

With a whoosh, we coasted down into an immense green valley. Hillside trees stood in bright yellow light while the sky behind them was smoky black and streaked with lightning. Clouds cast giant shadows over the land, and, in the distance, the sea was coming into view, blue and flecked with regular lines of foam.

As I took a bus from the airport into Georgetown, the main city on the island of Penang in Malaysia, a huge storm was blowing in. These were the luscious monsoon rains that came each afternoon with regularity after hours of clear, intense sunlight.

By the time we neared Georgetown, heavy raindrops had started to fall. The bus windows were hastily raised. The bracing smattering of water soon became thick sheets of warm rain and by the time the bus stopped at the wharf in Georgetown, the ocean could not be differentiated from the sky—all was a waterfall flowing in every direction.

This was right before the Gulf War—the original one. An international coalition of troops was massing in the Persian Gulf after Iraq's invasion and annexation of Kuwait. The press was reporting that Saddam Hussein's army was one of the most powerful in the world (the country's "third biggest tank army" was often cited) and everyone thought that the United States, spearheading the armed response, was really going to have a fight on its hands. Uncertainty reigned, as this was the first large-scale overt U.S. military deployment since Vietnam and the first such conflict that was taking on a worldwide aspect, as more and more nations became involved.

There was a growing sense that it would not end well for the U.S. The Americans had just about accepted that Vietnam had taught that their country could no longer prevail in overseas conflicts and that the death of any of its soldiers would cause a maelstrom of anti-war sentiment that would doom any war effort. Iraq's invasion was thought indicative of an uprising against U.S. dominance and that the U.S. was unavoidably sliding into a quagmire. Tourism around the world slowed as war tensions and uncertainty rose.

Anti-Americanism was peaking in many parts of the world, such as among the poorer Muslims in Malaysia. The bestselling book in Georgetown then was entitled something like *Saddam: Courageous Hero* in the local language. It was a biography of Saddam Hussein prominently on sale at every newsstand and bookstore. It was disturbing to see the hero worship of a person I had been taught was an evil dictator. I was somewhat apprehensive seeing this everywhere I turned, and, with the lack of tourists, I felt people were taking note of me as I walked through town in the pouring rain that day.

Georgetown had a small-town feeling to it: mostly two-storey shophouses at its core, with its suburbs consisting of vast areas of old Chinese-style mansions. A single multi-storey high-rise towered incongruously over the center of the city. It was the sort of structure that an enterprising local family probably had decided to develop long before there was any need for it.

The old Chinese mansions around the outskirts of the city were not just houses, but elaborate estates meant to demonstrate the wealth of the owners. Framed by a huge green mountain that reared up in the center of the island, they were built during a brief boom in rubber prices in the early twentieth century and quickly abandoned after the bottom fell out of the trade when artificial rubber replaced the natural kind. A few of the mansions were repurposed as foreign consulates, with one famously made into a branch of Kentucky Fried Chicken. Most were abandoned and covered with lichen and moss.

I was on the island of Penang for the once-familiar routine of those who worked in nearby Thailand. Every 90 days one had to exit the country, and, armed with the proper documents, obtain a new visa for Thailand at a consulate located in another country. It was an odd ritual, wherein expat workers saved up the money they made working month to month in Thailand and then exported it by spending it on a required visa trip in a nearby country.

This is why I was there—to obtain a visa from one of those suburban mansions that had been converted into a Thai consulate and that seemed to exist only to deal with the 30-40 workers a day from Thailand exporting their Thai salaries on a visa trip to Malaysia.

As usual, I tried to make sure I stayed in the absolute cheapest hotel to save money. The one I chose was a ruin of an old Chinese house, the shabbiest building on the street, unpainted, with tall stands of uncut weeds growing all around it. A crumbling wall stood in front and modern buildings pinned it in on both sides.

I vaguely recall either being warned against staying there or maybe it was just a premonition—like picking out the one obviously haunted house on the street to stay in.

Inside, in old-fashioned tropical style, the top of every wall was screened in so air could circulate freely throughout the building. This was assisted by old metal ceiling fans that were ever spinning above. It worked well, and the scent of green and of rain wafted through the rooms, along with the occasional smell of cigarette smoke at any hour of the day or night. The rest of my room was ancient unpainted wood. The bed was oddly placed in the exact center of the room, with a small table beside it. There was no other furniture. A single window faced out to a cement wall.

The shared bathroom at the end of the hall opened to an outdoor area on the roof of the building with concrete stalls. Each stall contained a large barrel filled with ice-cold water. To take a shower, one dipped a bowl into the barrel and then doused oneself. This was the method of bathing so common in many countries in the region. There was nothing like a shower in this refreshing way. After this, the modern continuous hot-water shower felt like a decadent invention, lacking the rush of a cold barrel-dipped splash of water.

I rented a bicycle and careened dangerously down the streets where new Malaysian-built Proton cars flowed non-stop day and night.

This was a country and a place that, as an American, I had never been taught about. Japan, Korea, the Philippines—that was Asia to an American. Malaysia's complex birth out of its initial merger with Singapore, its long-running communist insurgency, and its unique geography—two parts separated by hundreds of kilometers of the South China Sea—was unknown to me.

In the morning, I took a bus to a forest park nestled in the crux of green hills that rose up outside of town. Moments after I arrived, it rained thunderously, and, as I took refuge under a small shelter, the hills came alive with the sound of sudden streams and waterfalls. When the rain ceased, steam puffed off the tree trunks so intensely that I could see but a few feet in front of me and the air was so wet I was gasping in the humidity.

Later, at a Chinese temple where generations of family members were memorialized, half of a massive, undulating centipede was dropped on my shoulder by a bird or bat zooming overhead.

I tried fermented toddy made from palm fronds. Like all alcohol, it seemed to me to be desirable mainly as a social lubricant for those who could not stand themselves. I drank without much gusto while fending off the drug dealers who lurked everywhere in the area.

Malaysia proudly touted its "dadah means death" or "drugs mean death" policy. This meant the death penalty was imposed for possessing even small amounts of drugs. This harsh consequence was derided as savage by the other Westerners I worked with in Bangkok, and one might indeed have qualms about the harsh punishment only impacting the guilty poor and not the guilty rich. In my own homeland, drugs had ravaged the poor in particular, so it did not seem to me that Westerners had any special wisdom to dictate to Malaysia on the subject.

As the troop buildup to confront Saddam was ongoing, I heard, in both fluent and broken English, statements addressed to me like, "For America it will as another Vietnam, yes?" and "It is all over for the U.S." I heard this from drug dealers to businessmen that I met waiting for the bus. It broke my American conception of the world. From my sheltered perspective, and I think that of many of my compatriots, I felt that my U.S.-centric vision of the world was a commonsense one. Like the American of my day, I assumed there was good and bad and that everyone pretty much agreed on which was which.

It was thus surprising, if not shocking, to be met face to face with these diverging opinions. After seeing books lauding Saddam on every street corner and meeting those who relished the prospect of a crushing defeat for the U.S., I began telling people I was from Canada when asked. This had the effect of intensifying the conspiratorial nature of the comments I received — as if a Malaysian and a Canadian both naturally wished to chat about the coming collapse of the American empire.

That evening, I went to eat at a hotel outside the city center. This was away from the monolithic high-rise in the center of town. On the top floor of the hotel was a cocktail lounge that afforded an astounding view of the surrounding ocean and mainland as the sun set. Then I was beset by what I believe were prostitutes wearing old-fashioned ball gowns made from what looked like velvet drapes.

I fled the lounge and then ate dinner at the hotel banquet hall. Accompanying the dinner was a show featuring stunt motocross bicyclists from the U.S. who did amazing tricks on a very compact set of ramps. Then there was a chimpanzee act from Russia. It featured monkeys wearing prayer shawls and yarmulkes, clearly to ridicule Jewish people. The chimps sat on sacks of gold coins and did little dances. The impresario's Russian-language narration was interpreted to the crowd in the local language to great laughter and cheers.

Then I returned to my old Chinese hotel and decided to visit the pub that was attached to it. To get to the pub, one went along a hallway that had holes in the wall where the plaster had fallen away and where one could see into the pub beyond. The floors and walls of the pub were grey cement and it was as dank and shadowy as the hotel was open and airy. Two or three patrons were seated inside. No one stirred as I entered.

I sat down on a long bench that stretched along one wall. The main bar appeared to be a cabinet repurposed to be a bar. A man leaned on it from the other side, motionless and looking down at a newspaper. Behind him was a single bookcase with bottles and glasses. No one came to ask me for my order. Nothing about any of this looked like a real pub. It looked more like a dismal snack bar where everything had come to a standstill.

When I turned back, there was a person seated on the bench to my right. He was a gaunt man-boy with sallow eyes. He offered to sell me drugs. I refused. He said, "Then what are you doing here?"

I took another look around. The people seated on the other side of the room both were in a daze, eyes half-open, hardly moving.

"What are you here for?" he repeated. He had giant, watery, soulful eyes and was surreptitiously showing me something he held in his hand. I tried not to acknowledge it, but I knew it was some sort of drug. I was beginning to feel scared. I realized I was staying in an old wooden hotel connected to a drug den.

For some reason, I believed it would not be wise to jump up and run out immediately. I wanted to leave casually and not draw attention to myself. Maybe it was all a police setup. Surely they knew about this place. Maybe they were protecting it. These thoughts were racing through my mind when my concentration was broken by a man on the other side of the room moaning loudly. No one took any notice.

I do not know why I went in this direction, but I asked the man next to me what his religion was. He said he was a Muslim. I went into some diatribe about what his religious leaders would think of his life and him selling drugs. He was surprisingly receptive. He slowly twisted his body out of the scheming pose from which he had been offering me drugs, and then sat looking straight ahead.

He sighed, and I recall him earnestly telling me something about himself and his life — none of which I can recall now. I wish I could remember what he had said, but as he spoke, I was becoming more and more distracted. I thought, "I need to just get up and get out of here." Then, from the pub entrance, two indistinct people appeared and stared at me suspiciously.

This spooked me. I stood up and walked out as casually as I could. I went back to my room. There was nowhere else to go and

I half expected police to come knocking on my door and then find I had been set up. But that did not happen.

That night it was both pleasantly humid and cool, as a new storm was starting to pass over. I lay on the bed and it was quiet, save for the fan whirring away overhead. The next morning I washed away my fears with barrel-dipped water, then successfully retrieved my new visa and flew away from the island.

It may appear that I have portrayed Penang, and Malaysia, by extension, as lawless or sleazy or menacing, but nothing could be further from the truth. Malaysia, along with nearby Singapore, is among the most orderly and praiseworthy societies in the region. In spite of Malaysia's casual anti-Semitism and virtual one-party states, its crime rates, cleanliness and human development would certainly be the envy of many nations.

I went back to Malaysia many times—always on Thailand's perplexing "visa runs" to spend the money I made in Thailand in Malaysia.

On one of those subsequent trips, I took a train down the verdant Malay Peninsula. The fresh pungent scent of oil, apparently from the machinery of the locomotive, wafted into the open windows of the carriage. Where every kilometer alongside the train tracks in Thailand is lined by human development, in less densely populated Malaysia, the tracks wind through powerfully green jungles. I was seated next to a Zoroastrian from Iran and he told me of his religion. It was the story of yet another man, like Buddha, Jesus or Muhammad, who mistook their own internal struggle as a prescription for all mankind.

Georgetown was as peaceful as always. It had not yet experienced the growth that would soon make the island of Penang one of the largest computer hard-drive manufacturing centers in the world.

Once in town, I saw magazines and advertisements everywhere touting a new movie—*Jurassic Park*. I was eager to see it.

The theater I found showing the film was a classic single-screen theater with an old-fashioned flashing-lights marquee. It was midafternoon and all the other people buying tickets were high-school age girls wearing full head-to-toe hijabs that only showed their faces. I thought they must be from a nearby school that had just let out for the day.

Inside the theater, they floated here and there, their gowns billowing. Occasionally one would emit a quickly suppressed titter of laughter, but they were mostly stony-faced and dignified.

To my surprise, the main theater level was already full and I was herded up to the balcony. The theater was grand and spacious, and the balcony was an old type, so rarely seen now, huge and steep, that felt like it was tilting down to the screen below.

I was seated in the middle of the balcony, surrounded by school girls attired in identical hijabs. No one acknowledged me. I ended up feeling rather self-conscious and out of place in this otherwise uniform sea of people.

Then the lights dimmed and the red curtains were drawn back from the screen and *Jurassic Park* began. It was indeed a classic film, focusing on the awe and wonder of the dinosaurs, where later, lesser filmmakers saw prehistoric beasts only as an excuse for action and horror.

I was fascinated at how vocal the audience became during the film, at first bursting out in squeals at exciting parts, then graduating to yells and finally to full-throated screams during the most thrilling scenes. This was accompanied by the girls grabbing those to either side and shaking them with excitement.

I was afforded the same treatment. Girls on either side of me first grabbed my forearms and eventually my upper arms, shaking and screaming during the exciting parts. I was treated just like another one of the gang.

The audience increasingly became a taut ball of attention, watching raptly and then letting loose with screams and shaking those next to them once the thrilling action began. Before long I was shouting too at the exciting parts and fully living the excitement and tension. This must be what a filmmaker wishes for in the appreciation of their art—full emotion and abandon to what they have created.

By the time the movie got to the part where the two children were hiding from dinosaurs in the kitchen, my ears were ringing from the squeals of the audience, my arms were sore and I saw some of the girls on the lower level of the theater jumping out of their seats and running up and down the aisles in excitement.

Finally, the credits rolled, the lights came up and everyone filed out, again in a dignified fashion, robes gently flowing in the waning sunlight.

There are not too many times, if ever, when strangers in an audience experience such abandon. Maybe it is only school girls and reckless travelers abroad who are ever able to do it.

The next day I discovered dark bruises had formed on both of my arms where I had been grabbed and shaken. For a few days it was a tangible reminder of that afternoon in a theater in Penang.

THE END OF THE ALLEY

EVEN soon afterwards, he had forgotten her. That is how he was. If he did sometimes remember her, he altered her to become small, squat, brown—not worth it—and he became the hero of the tale, taking action to move things along.

He met her at a photo shop. This was a business that developed film from cameras, and at one time thousands of these shops operated across Thailand. Every major street had at least one Kodak and one Fuji shop—and the occasional Konica too. Then one day there was no need to develop physical film and they all vanished.

These shops developed millions of photo of temples—the same photos tourists took for generations. Only rarely was a photo taken of the urban city streets or an average person on a bus hurrying to work. All over the world there must be photos stored away in boxes of the same temples at sunset and girls dancing in traditional costumes. The only indication of when they were originally taken — today or decades ago — is from the slow yellowing of the photos themselves.

His photos were no different, but to his own eye they were unique and impossibly special — examples of odd things that odd people made in places far away. His own fixation on the exotic of any land he visited created an implicit understanding that normal standards of propriety did not apply.

She worked in the photo shop. Although he had altered the details, somewhere, deep in his mind, the reality of it was still there. She was young and attractive, another in the legions of such women. There were so many that it made the starving Western man undiscerning. Where he came from, everything had to be earned and begged for and justified — and what there was to have was rare, which meant that any opportunity had to be immediately exploited.

In a place where a typical workaday girl was open to meet and love a foreign man, even one not so attractive or rich such as he, it made him grab for these supposedly rare opportunities out of habit. It made him feel full and handsome.

So he took her to see a movie. It was something scary and he loved movies, but like all movies, it was forgettable — something fanciful and an attempt to titillate. It did not cost much, though.

Then there was a nighttime Bangkok taxi ride, careening along, lit inside by an array of lights from the meter — a red dot and a number indicating the fare — the dot forever blinking out a warning to those who never see it. He was looking at her and she at him and the taxi was suddenly rushing down one of the long twisting alleys that projected off every main street.

He was already starting to expect this. Anxiously going back to her place. Still, every time it started to happen, it was amazing to him.

The long alley zigged and zagged with no reason. The road sometimes was crimped to a single lane where a motorcycle was parked at an angle so that it stuck out into the road. The driver no doubt was also in a hurry and in his haste did not care about parking properly.

Nearly all of those long alleys went nowhere. They came to dead ends at the canals that lay across the city. Bangkok should have been a city of bridges, but for reasons he never knew, the Thais were content to let these streets end at brackish waters. The alleys were sometimes many kilometers long with only one way in and out. The sides of the alleys were lined by tall jealous walls capped with broken glass set into concrete.

She lived in a little hovel of an apartment—three stories of boxes meant to hold the provincial workers that made up most of the common workforce of Bangkok.

On the way to her room, they passed a guy who followed them for a few steps—a young, dark, strongly built Thai man with an expression so odious, so suspicious, that he must surely have been harmless. One who wished him harm would surely hide it.

In the room they sat on a mat and she shrank into a small, wan thing, but now with an almost devilish smile. He sat and saw his own legs as they extended from his shorts. They looked mottled and had a sickening flesh color in the light. He did not want to look at his flat squat legs. His eyes fled to her and then around the room again.

Nothing on the walls. A bed mat. An ice bucket. It was a room for people from other parts of the country to stay in when they worked in the big city. None of these people ever moved to the city permanently, even if they lived in Bangkok their whole working life. Before anything else, they were residents of their own far-off province—a place with its own specific foods and sometimes dialects. They were foreigners in the capital of their own nation.

It was inevitable that Bangkok became the nation's singular city. It was centered in the middle of the country at the mouth of its main river valley. It was the place where most of the best-paying jobs were, and, despite campaigns to keep people from outlying provinces from coming, the nation was a funnel and Bangkok was the center of the country and labor flowed to it. It was opportunity.

On weekends and holidays, workers in Bangkok would repair to their family homes in the country, riding all night on the bus.

During the week they stayed in the economical concrete boxes, working and saving money to send back home each month to care for their aged parents. He did not know this yet, and the way the Thais lived seemed depressing to him.

He had been funneled into Bangkok as well, into a slightly bigger room with a few more possessions. Sometimes he felt the depression of living in a bare room in a big city with no end in sight, but he consoled himself that he was far and above these regional laborers—like the one who was kneeling across from him on this mat in the dim room in the middle of Siam. He thought it was a wonderful age when things just happened and a young man never said no to any opportunity in a young woman's room.

Something was being chopped or hammered outside—no doubt by the sinister man.

She uncurled her hand. In this light it was as discolored as his legs had looked. Her hand was empty, but she indicated that she wanted payment.

Suddenly a noxious cynicism arose in him. He had expected something for nothing, of course, as he was a young man. He did not think it was just this—a transaction—although he would have run away afterwards anyway. Then he felt anger, because this was not about him, but about the trade and transactions of the city he could not escape.

The girl said something and the Thai man appeared at the door, rearing up, standing there in overt sinisterness.

Almost without thinking he stood up and walked out of the room, with the rapid walk of one who wants to run, but dares not show he needs to run, walking past the sinister man and away from the wan woman kneeing on the mat.

He dared not look back. This would show uncertainty, inviting attack. He was also aware he was at the end of the long twisting street, bounded by its high walls and broken glass. The only way out was the way he had come. He hurried.

He worried that he might turn the wrong way and end up at a dead end. He should not have gone down that alley. He thought he was being followed. Just go on and get away from this. It had worked thus far.

Finally, he sensed he was not being followed and broke into a run. He was alone again. He knew he must be drawing closer to the main road where he had first entered the alley.

Then he was finally there. It was windy and cool in the thin, even sheen of the street lights. He was out. He had made the right decision, he thought, in running, but he was not entirely sure.

The next day he went back to pick up his photos. The attendant said, "I am surprised to see you here."

"Oh?" he said.

"She said her boyfriend caught you together and beat you up."

"No," he said, trying to act amused and unshaken.

He left the shop and never went back there again.

GETTING AN AIDS TEST

I was careful to make sure the airline reservations were right. It was all done on the phone back then, and I was always a careful person. Still, random niggling things happened, typically at inopportune times, which could be embarrassing and potentially disastrous.

One time the return reservations were mysteriously cancelled. It was only by chance that I caught this. I could never rest easy, because I was surrounded by unseen things that would mess up the most carefully considered plans.

This was when I was acting as a sort of travel guide for my Thai boss and his family. I accompanied them on their frequent trips overseas to handle the niceties of checking in, driving a rental car and sometimes preventing them from being cheated. I made the arrangements, paid for everything with the company card, and intercepted the pushy and cheating scum that Asian travelers attracted when they were on holiday.

My boss was a man of some success and means. He did not like dealing with annoying white people and had the resources to bring me along to be a barrier between him and having to deal with the pushy New Yorkers or fussy Frenchmen or exasperated Italians, who I did observe grew more demonstrative when dealing with generally reticent Thais like my boss and his family.

One time in London, I was warned by the hotel concierge about a group of people targeting Asians. These people can apparently no longer be referred to by their traditional name, so I will leave it at that.

That very day in London, we were in a large department store when a gang of them came right at us, tunneling through racks of coats from multiple directions to surround and attempt to rob my boss's wife and daughter. The attackers were all short of stature and barely visible above the sea of clothes that rustled as they passed through. I was standing a few meters away and had to rush over to where it was happening. I threw them off and blocked them one by one as they grabbed at purses and ripped at our pockets.

As I was punching and kicking them away, I lifted up my knee and one hit me square on the kneecap then immediately fell back, apparently knocked out cold. We were shouting for help as this was happening and store clerks had rushed over, but the gang eerily vanished into the clothing as if they had never been there at all. Even the one who was knocked unconscious was gone—I caught a glimpse of his feet as he was dragged away under the racks of clothes.

After that, I had a feeling they were always nearby, lurking just out of sight. These were the strangely random events that happened unexpectedly. It made me worry about many things.

Being a young man of a certain age and experience, and living when there was no treatment or cure for AIDS, I became concerned about this peril of the age that I lived in. I had not really done anything unsafe, but I could not really know for sure. I think I was typical or even less than typical for the day, considering my ability to attract and seduce verses my age and urges.

It is undoubtedly difficult today to understand what it was like to grow up in that era of a new and fatal venereal disease. It was both a plague and a taboo. When one came of age, there was dread instead of joy.

From where I was raised in conservative middle America, religious types embraced the AIDS epidemic. The entire narrative of AIDS was pushed as proof of traditional religious views about God's infallibility concerning sexuality and gender.

This was probably a natural trend of thinking in the 1980s, just as the U.S. was pulling back from the unbridled liberalism of previous decades. Religious leaders worked hard to make me feel that this new plague was reaching out for me personally and could hit anyone who had sex out of wedlock. It was not just about far-off New Yorkers or gay people. This new plague was all about my generation, they assured me. It could hit any young person during their fumbling first time at sinning even in the countryside. Without close adherence to the traditional ways that I had been taught about in the Bible, I would surely become infected. "One time is all it takes," they said.

Eventually, I sensed similar entreaties from liberal activists. They also made sure that I knew that this was something that fully applied to me — it was not just for gays and intravenous drug users. They surely felt that if society at large did not fear AIDS, it might be left to linger as an ailment of a fringe minority.

That was the horror of sex that everyone across the political spectrum wanted me to experience — or at least it seemed so at the time. All sides were working hard to ensure everyone knew they were at risk and that anyone could be infected — and probably very easily.

It even twisted the vocabulary. Instead of a venereal disease, it became an STD. If nothing can really be done, at least we can update the name.

Incurable diseases were talked of in hushed tones, but this was one that was wrapped in religious morality plays and even smug satisfaction that this plague validated religious teachings. After all, when one heard that a person had died of AIDS, one never thought that the person must have been an intravenous drug user.

So I was in Thailand at the peak of this incurable scourge. In that place, HIV was viewed as part of the dirty West and thus unable to really be a threat to the cloistered world of the Thais. It was a disease of the lowly and dirty who were karmically unlucky. Thais offered their wisdom that one should not even try being gay. In those days being gay was thought of as an activity. "If you try it, you might like it," and that meant death.

In Thailand, charms were touted to prevent HIV and allow condomless activity. There were also natural herbal remedies proved — by anecdote only — to cure the disease. I am sure many depended on these talismans and herbal remedies because there was nothing else.

On one hand, I had no real reason to think I was infected, but it was supposed to be prudent to get tested from time to time. More than anything else, I was increasingly being influenced by the constant entreaties of those who wanted me to think one thing or another about the disease.

After all, Thailand had spectacularly high levels of HIV infections. The lure of the place and its tourism was based on its lascivious nightlife. Rumors spread that in certain provinces 20 percent of new army recruits were found to be infected. Whether true or not, the dread was rising. It was an icy, needling fear, the kind that came when one woke up in the middle of the night.

So the necessity to have an "AIDS test" slowly grew in me. In later years it was emphasized that such a thing was properly called an "HIV test" as it was a test for the presence of the virus and not the resulting condition. At that time, with the lack of any treatment, having HIV meant one would eventually get AIDS. Without a viable treatment, there seemed to be little distinction made between the two back then.

So in the milieu of the time, I felt that it would be prudent to be tested. Then this grew to urgency and worry, and finally an almost panicked resignation that reasoned, "How could I not be infected?" Like every young man, I imagined that I was in the center of my generation and my time. This meant that the things that were happening — that could happen — would certainly happen to me.

Getting the test in Thailand meant first providing a copy of one's passport. In the event of a positive result, one could be expelled from the country. An infection was something that insurance did not cover. Then there was explaining it to one's family or the stress of holding the secret.

Since it was not practical to be tested in Thailand and I wanted to keep my options open in the event of a bad result, I needed to look for a chance to be tested.

The next month, I was escorting my boss's family to Disney World in Florida. This was the chance.

After flying in, I drove them into the Disney World area and to our hotel. As usual, it was not right. They required something luxurious and refined. That night, the place we were pulling into was a low-rise, old-style hotel. I realized that the Disney reservation operator I made the reservations with had misled me. I had specifically asked for high-class, luxurious hotel rooms. The operator had assured me the hotel was indeed luxurious. It clearly was not.

Sometimes this happened. When dealing with reservations people in the U.S. and mentioning "wanting the best," I was purposely directed to a completely unsuitable hotel or restaurant. I was not sure if the reservations people were deliberately steering me wrong to punish my elitism or if they were actually unable to judge how one accommodation might be considered superior to another. Or maybe it was just dumb bad luck. That worried me.

As this was running through my mind, we drove into the parking lot, and incredibly, as if to punctuate the unsuitability of the hotel, several police cars with lights blazing were there. A drunken fighting family was being physically separated by the police.

My mind was a blank as I walked in a daze to check the room while my boss and his family remained safely locked in the car. There was always one room for the family and another for me and there was nothing more pleasant after a long flight than to get everyone settled in for the night. Now I was beginning to think it would be a long time before we would have suitable accommodations.

I unlocked the door of the hotel room. The floor was covered in outdoor plastic carpeting, clearly designed for a rough and tumble family spending all of their time coming back and forth from the pool.

I could see that this motel, deep inside Disney territory, was designed to evoke the roadside inns of the past. It actually possessed an interesting nostalgia factor, with slender hanging gold lamps and kitschy artwork. Then another ruckus arose from the drunken family and the police. I closed the door without turning on the lights. My Thai family would not be able to appreciate the retro irony of the room, and I suppressed a chuckle as I returned to the car and passed by the fighting, white trash family — the dad now in handcuffs. Welcome to Florida.

My Thai family expected rooms with champagne waiting for them and I had come up with this. It was another unsettling annoyance for me, having booked such a weirdly unsuitable place.

After more phone calls, I finally obtained rooms in a proper hotel. Once in my own room, I immediately pulled out the phone book and found a clinic nearby where I could be tested. Soon I was at the clinic. I barely remember driving there.

As I sat on the metal table in the examination room and smelled the antiseptic, I gradually began to see grey chunks floating before my eyes and then more and more, until I interrupted the doctor's spiel about the dangerous diseases of Bangkok by saying, "May I... ah... lie down here... I have to faint," and I collapsed sideways on the table on which I was sitting.

Coming out of it was the worst. It was a frustrating physical nightmare. It is consciousness, but no brain. I was aware of being, but did not know my name or where I was. I should have been somewhere.

I tried to place myself, but every thought slid away — there was nowhere to put them. It was a twilight of nothingness when I knew there should be something. Then I whizzed back and heard the blood rushing in my ears, the air conditioner, the swish of cars and the sickening background noise that made up the world I was in.

The doctor said, "It's ok, you've had a lot on your mind lately," as if he was reading my thoughts.

Blood was taken and I lay down for 20 minutes to recover a bit from my fainting. At the reception desk I asked, "How much will the tests be?" The receptionist replied, "He's going to have them test for everything, so it may be a lot."

Suddenly, I saw the chunks again before my eyes. I staggered to a chair and crumpled. Moments later I awoke with a start, since my head had fallen backwards in an unnatural, painful position. I realized I was slumped awkwardly in the chair. A small tank of oxygen was wheeled out and I breathed it for a while. Other than that, little attention was given to the obviously distressed person who had just been tested. It was as if it were proper punishment for my lasciviousness.

I was getting scared. Having a physical reaction to the mere possibility of infection meant that this involuntary response could slip out at any time. All my attempts to put things in their place and rationalize them were swept away by my mind that wanted me to know how much I really feared the possibilities.

I drove back trembling, but gradually felt better as I put distance between myself and where I had left my blood.

The next day, I escorted the family through Disney World — Adventureland, Frontierland, and Tomorrowland. I was my chipper self and I do not think anyone was aware I was beside myself waiting for the test results. Inside, I felt as if I were on a rollercoaster at the moment it starts to rush down from the highest peak.

I was anxious to get back to the clinic. I was worried that I would not be able to have time to go back. For some reason, it felt imperative that I not make any excuse, true or not, that I needed to go. I felt that I needed to find some time on my own and just go without saying anything — as if any excuse I made to go would be seen through immediately.

Some people might face their own mortality early on — a cancer scare or some other deadly disease of a malfunctioning body — but most can blissfully skate on, decade after decade, without giving a thought to the unpleasant future. Death is best when it is seen as an unlucky quality or vexing habit in others — something that should never have to be considered in the now.

This fatal venereal disease, and the taboos it was supposed to embody, and the messages I was being fed about it, offered an opportunity for everyone of my generation to face the possibility that their greatest joys could result in an ignominious end. For those who wanted to maintain the illusion of youthful invulnerability and the ability to spurn religious dictums, it was a dreadful smack in the face.

So I found a moment a few days later and returned to the dismal clinic. The low sodium street lights cast a sickening orange glow that was anemic and restricted.

I thought of the international schools in Thailand that supposedly kept their foreign students from the pernicious nightlife by telling them that most Thai people were infected with HIV. I thought of the doctor who told me, while taking blood, that Thailand was not a place one should visit these days.

I went into the same examination room and sat back on the same table I had fainted on last time. I sat there and gasped, feeling woozy, as I waited for someone to return with my test results.

"This is what life is about," I thought. The baby boomers had once lived with sexual abandon and some probably still did. I hated their free love. I relished the fact that in the 1980s they transformed into vacuous yuppies and their beliefs and hippie ways were upended by conservatism. They had said there was abandon, but there was no abandon. Their free love was something my generation would never experience. Even if a cure was discovered tomorrow, it was already spoiled. It had become too serious and consequential. Just the words "infection" and "positive" would forever have sour rings. It did not seem fair.

So it came time to receive the results. By then I was unable to think logically and linearly. My mind was a disorganized stream, just barely able to anticipate knowing the results.

Two people entered the room. I did not know what that meant. They went on about something I could not concentrate on and I cut them off to remind them that I wanted the results.

They first made me sign document after document both from the clinic and the State of Florida about one thing after another. Indemnification. That I had been read my rights. And so on.

Then the two went into a canned spiel about AIDS — the options and free services and hospices available, counseling, and lack of curative drugs.

I protested — at one point clawing at the paperwork one of them was holding in an attempt to get at the results.

They pulled back the paperwork from my grasp and even seemed pleased. No! It was regulation or state law, I cannot remember which, and I was required to hear the disclaimers verbally beforehand so I knew the medical options and my rights before I was permitted to see my results.

I wondered what this meant. The consequences sprang back into view and the horror rose. I thought that it must mean that I was positive and they were saying this so I knew the resources available before I heard the dire news.

I found myself flat out on the examination table. I did not remember lying down. I again asked what this meant. Did they know I was positive? Is that why they were saying all this?

They again said it was regulation or maybe state law — I could not really focus in on what they were saying. My mind was swimming, but they did not say they knew what the results were. This must mean something. It was torture. It all must mean something.

If it were positive, I had about five years, I thought. I did not think I could go blithely back to Disney World and pretend like all was ok. I could never tell my family. The middle class in the U.S. blames victims, because they live in a world that is too safe. They cannot imagine bad things happening to an innocent person, and thus the victim is blamed. I felt I was to blame as my mind raced.

Finally, I was solemnly handed a simple sealed envelope. I was so engrossed in seeing it that when I started to carefully open it, I realized that the room was empty. Apparently regulations or state law required that sinners face this alone.

I was negative.

I reread it very carefully several times and I think I actually rubbed my eyes. Yes, I was seeing it right, it was negative.

My mind was still cluttered by the long list of official pronouncements that had preceded me being allowed to see my results. It had been made needlessly agonizing, but then such torment came with so many things in life.

I slid off the table and stood unsteadily, all alone. I wondered if those documents I had signed indemnified them if I fainted now and cracked my head open. They knew I had fainted last time.

I left the building. No one spoke to me or even looked at me.

When I got back to the hotel, I examined the test results one more time to be sure. I found that I had grasped the papers and the envelope in my hand at some point. It was a mashed ball, with my finger marks clearly discernible.

The tests showed only that I was low in potassium, which, in conjunction with my general nervousness, could have resulted in my fainting.

The telling of this experience might seem more fraught and dire than necessary. Today there are treatments and HIV is no longer a death sentence, but on the day in which it unfolded, I keenly felt the cruel need of my culture to impress the lesson of this virus on those being tested. And I still do.

All this ignited and intensified my long-boiling hypochondria. When those I knew did die, from this or that, it reinforced the idea that just because I was a hypochondriac, it did not mean I was not really sick and dying.

Future trips I took remained beset with peculiar gremlins that messed up my travel plans — mysteriously cancelled reservations and flight times that changed without warning. At least, that was my impression. Things tended to happen and I could never really relax for long.

However, on that trip back from Disney World, I carefully checked the tickets and reservations, and everything occurred exactly as planned, without further incident.

THE REAL AND
THE STRANGE

THE building where I worked in Bangkok was thick with curses and spells, as I am sure was the case in many Thai businesses with their repressed office politics. A common curse was writing a person's name on a piece of tape and putting it on a stair where it would be stepped on all day. Thais insult with the foot and stepping on a person's name is rudely cursing them.

More than once, I noticed my own name on a tiny piece of tape on a step. I knew this was from the boss's several good-for-nothing relatives at the company who were forever irked by my unwanted innovations and attempts at accountability concerning the large amounts of cash the business brought in daily.

The first time I saw my name on a tape on the stairs and knew what it was, I removed it and jokingly showed it to my boss to prove it had no real meaning to me.

He told me I should not have taken it off. Since I did not believe in curses, he reasoned, they had no power over me and thus it did not matter if it was on the step. If the person who put it there noticed I removed it and that I did not care about the curse, they might be tempted to try other more effective or harmful ways to make me sorry. So by all means, he told me, I should put it back on the stair and let the person be satisfied they were getting their revenge.

So I put it back. I hope it made them happy or "satisfied," as the Thais would put it.

Another time, a strange lady was hired at the company. I cannot now remember for what position. I think it was something like office manager. She was beautiful and often dressed in black. In her interview, she not only demonstrated she was competent, but also that she had the right personality for managing people.

Almost immediately after she started work, she became combative and even provoking, especially problematic for the rest of the Thais staff, who traditionally favor non-confrontational attitudes in their worklife. She became a very negative force in the office and even I began avoiding her.

Then she, myself and several others in the company went on a trip to Laos, along with a delegation of police officers. This was to explore the option of setting up various businesses. Of course, Laos being a "People's Democratic Republic" meant that nothing was straightforward, and thus much negotiation via mutual ties between Thai and Laotian police was required.

During the trip, the wife of a senior policeman with us sensed something weird about the abrasive office manager who dressed in black. When the policeman's wife got back to Bangkok, she sent some special policemen, who were trained as empaths, to investigate her.

The empaths were a team of what might more commonly be called psychics. Thais were loathe to let others — particularly Westerners — know of this integral part of Thai police investigative work. The fear was that haughty Westerners who liked to lecture would almost certainly deride police "fortune tellers" as a worthless superstition.

The empaths reported back that the lady in black lived in an old house which was also a portal to another dimension — the spirit world. This made her a kind of witch and very dangerous.

Some months later I ended up firing her, with no repercussions, so her power was probably not that strong.

Another time, I dreamed that I entered my boss's house and sensed it was filled with demons. There were so many demons that objects in the house trembled with their possession. In the dream, I went down into the basement and determined that was where most of the demons were. They grew fewer in number as I walked up through the levels of the house, with the most powerful and controlling demon residing in an electrical device or light socket at the very top of the house. I also sensed that the demons (or whatever they were) could be cast out temporarily, but the only way to permanently expel them was to find a policeman who used to be a monk or holy man. He would know the right procedure to get rid of them.

I dreamed this three times. I do not know what to attribute it to — staring at too many temples, a strange surfacing of instinct, or too much sun — but it was certainly strange and specific.

I had no intention of telling anyone, but one day the boss and his wife were speaking in concerned tones to some friends and a policeman who I knew was also an empath. Over the previous months, I had noticed an accumulation of magic masks, along with other traditional Thai bric-a-brac — all blessed by monks — that were placed around my boss's business premises and house. Sacred strings were repeatedly strung around his house as a sign of blessing and protection.

My boss began to tell me of his bad fortune. His business and construction plans were having endless problems and he was being sued and did not trust his own lawyers.

As my boss was telling me of his travails, I paused one last time in my supposed world of rationality where I was taught to fashionably scoff at religion and superstitious beliefs. Then I told him of my dream about the demons and the cursed object at the top of the house. He, and the small group he was seated with, did not appear amazed or skeptical, but instead were intensely interested.

"Why didn't you tell me this before?" my boss shot back at me, almost angrily.

"Because I don't believe any of this," I said, and we all laughed a bit. "If you hadn't told me about your bad fortune, I wouldn't have said anything at all."

Late that night, I received an excited call from my boss. He had checked and there was an amulet that had been placed in a juncture box at the peak of the attic space of his house. It had a curse dabbed in talcum powder around it. We were both amazed.

That someone tried to curse him was not too surprising. He was completely good-hearted, but was frequently short with staff and the contractors he dealt with, calling people late at night with demanding and involved ideas that they had to implement right away. It was possible that someone might have been pushed too far and wished him bad fortune.

The next day, I was told that there was indeed a policeman who was once a forest hermit for a time and claimed to know the correct process to handle the amulet's threat. Apparently some rituals were performed, the amulet was removed and the bad fortune abated. This incident gave me the reputation of being something of a seer and I am sure the tale grew in its retelling, giving pause to those who might dare to curse me with the old tape-on-the-stairs routine.

I cherished such strange incidents. Believing in any of them meant believing in magical things, curses, and fully clothed people in another veiled world waiting until I was suddenly able to see them. I admit that it is all preposterous, but the mind and the city seek to create satisfying mysteries.

Tramping down the sidewalks to work each day, trying not to step in a puddle or brush a live electric wire left hanging down, I felt the yearning behind the geometric world. Deep in the night, at the end of some dark Bangkok alley, things squirm, releasing their magic, an affront to the rational universe we have created. This is very satisfying.

On another evening, I was walking home, my white shirt smudged with pencil lead and daubed with sweat. The shirt had retreated back to its natural state of being wrinkled, as the toil of the day erased all attempts to create creases and smoothness.

This was in the Sao Ching Cha district in the old part of Bangkok. It was street after street thick with shophouses and older, earlier-era wooden houses wedged in between them. It was canyons lined with the energy of Thai enterprise — restaurants and groceries with the owners living above them, travel agencies, photo developing shops, printing houses, shops selling Buddhas and other votive items, and open-air mechanics' shops, black with oil from drained engines and with a welding arc continually blazing, its dry metallic smell wafting out onto the sidewalk. Neon-colored fluorescent bulbs burned over food stalls along the sidewalk and insects buzzed. As long as I did not stop, they would not get me.

I turned down a street where I would soon pass Wat Mahan Pharam Worawihan. This was a temple — one of the endless virtually anonymous and interchangeable places created to allow people to accrue merit to ensure good things came to them. They sometimes housed the infirm and were a place to drop off unwanted dogs. Water dripped onto the white stone walls of the temple grounds, and moss and black lichen grew in many places.

It was about 7 p.m. and the street by the temple had fallen unusually quiet. Even the traffic was suddenly absent. Three young boys were walking towards me from the opposite direction on the sidewalk. They wore short brown pants and white short-sleeved shirts like school children did, but in an old-fashioned style that made me notice them. They were extremely skinny. One was holding a small brown ball. It was odd, made of reeds like the old original balls used for the game of *takraw* — a sort of kick volleyball.

When they were about two meters from me, they turned and entered the temple through a gate. A moment later I looked through the gate as I passed, but there was no one there. I stopped and looked again, and walked through the gate and into the grounds of the temple. There was no sign of anyone.

This was intriguing. I wanted to make sure I knew where they had gone. I did not want to be half-sure about what I saw. I checked on either side of the gate, but found nowhere they could have hidden.

Inside the temple walls was a wide field of bare earth surrounded by temple buildings and some open-air pavilions. The area was deserted. I checked around the thick wall on either side of the gate. The wall was too tall to climb and came to a peak, so no one could walk on it.

The boys had stepped through the gate only seconds before I did. I did not feel frightened or even amazed. I was just puzzled that there appeared to be boys walking along and then they were gone. Back out on the street, the sound of traffic returned and all was bustling again as usual. Somehow the experience was so peaceful I did not think of it much for the next few months. It was just another weird thing that I began to expect.

A year later, I was walking by the same temple, but this time it was in the morning and I was going in the opposite direction. On this occasion, quite a few people were walking along the sidewalk. It was right before 8 a.m. and everyone was hurrying to get to work or school on time.

A bow-legged man was walking towards me. He was old and brown, the kind of homeless or mentally ill person who often lived in temple grounds. A young school girl was walking a few paces behind him. The temple gate jutted out onto the sidewalk and stood between us.

As I started to pass by the gate, the old man moved out of sight to the corner formed by the high wall of the temple and the gate. The school girl continued towards me, passing me and continuing on.

To my amazement, as I passed by the gate and looked to where the old man should have been, he was not there. The corner formed by the gate and wall was empty. The wall and gate were tall — there was no way anyone could have scrambled over them. Other people walked along the street, going about their business, but I was sure that a moment before, a slow-moving old man was on the sidewalk too. Now he was gone.

The nearly forgotten memories of the vanishing boys came to mind. I do not know why their memory had receded so far back. Maybe it was because I could not explain it. I was certain about what I saw, but I could not really believe in what I had seen.

My boss told me that the visions of the boys and the old man at the temple were a spiritual gift and I should reciprocate by presenting offerings at the temple. I intended to do so, but never did.

Another intriguing early experience was in Ayutthaya, the capital of one of the former kingdoms of Siam. It was a day trip from Bangkok past open fields. Just a few concrete shophouses were beginning to edge up to the eastern boundary of the old city.

Ayutthaya used to be further away, but as Bangkok grew outward, Ayutthaya grew closer. Today, the ancient part of the city is hemmed in on all sides in the style of the new Asian towns — anxiously built concrete with no ornamentation.

Centuries before, the grand armies of Ayutthaya and Burma fought back and forth battles. Many stone monuments still stand that commemorate the deeds of those who once went off to war on the backs of elephants.

As an American, anything approaching 200 years old seemed extremely old. In my home country, most things 200 years old are on its east coast. On its west coast, outside of a few ancient Spanish missions, most old buildings are 150 years old or less. So the great antiquity of Ayutthaya and the massive stone ruins were a singularly compelling attraction to me.

I occasionally drove my old Fiat up to the ruins on a Friday afternoon just to wander around. After becoming familiar with the major sites, I started exploring the few that were not marked on maps and still overgrown. One was a small complex of ruins south of the ancient city's northern moat. I had glimpsed them through trees from the road. These overgrown ruins were on a much smaller scale than the towering ones promoted to tourists.

A partially broken gate at the site was open and I drove in, almost getting stuck in the powdered red dirt that the city was built upon. No signs identified what the ruins once were.

I looked around warily, as I knew the reputation of the area. For decades, bandits were front-page news. This was when the Thai state did not yet have control over all the corners of the land. Self-interested men took advantage of the remoteness of many areas and were mythologized as rebellious heroes. By the 1980s, the last vestiges of the bandit culture had been stamped out, but the first tourist brochures I read on Ayutthaya still had notices explaining to tourists that they could rest easy as the monuments were safe from banditry—even the outlying ones. In the present day, fears of bandits are distant in Thailand, replaced with fears of falling concrete beams from multi-billion dollar mass transit projects.

On that day at that place, it was dusk and the sky was beginning to glow furiously. The red brick and beige stones of the ruins became crisp and textured in the light. I walked around a vaguely pyramidal-shaped structure. It was really more of a mound of blocks in ever-ascending stacks. What it was originally was impossible to tell. After one circuit, I continued to walk around it for some reason. I began to be able to see, out of the corner of my left eye, a figure moving along with me. It was wearing unusual clothing and carrying either a staff or maybe a sickle. In the dying light, the colors of its clothing were muted. I suddenly thought this must be a leftover bandit that I had roused from his late-afternoon sleep.

The figure was four meters away from me and several steps back. I cautiously turned my head to see it more clearly. To my surprise, it was gone. Until that moment, I had not imagined it was not an actual person shadowing me. I continued walking, and, as I did, the figure in the corner of my eye returned. I turned, and immediately it was gone. I started walking and it was there again.

The figure walked like it was tiptoeing in larger than normal strides. It wore a ragged garment, perhaps a tunic, and something horizontal across its shoulders, like shoulder pads. I never got a clear view of what it was carrying, but it looked like a spear with a long blade or maybe a misshapen staff.

I walked all the way around the ruins again while watching the figure — always in the corner of my eye. As the last light of the sun went away, I perceived the figure was fading too. I was not able to determine if it saw me. I had no sensation of fear. It was just an odd event, maybe brought on by my own wonder. I did not know for sure and still do not.

Thailand was unerringly physical despite its exotic temples and locale. Its heat was persistent. Its dust was everywhere, and it was, like so many developing places, becoming encased in concrete — newly dried, firm or crumbling. The legions of taxi drivers with their scowls, office workers standing in lurching buses, and slow-moving shop clerks — all the passive, taut people — surely must be insisting that there is something more. Every place made of angular concrete desired to be broken so that all could see the shining justice that must certainly underlie the sweat and the pain of walking through the hard world.

Sometimes, even now, I can see a thing at the far periphery of my vision, watching me. Then I turn and nothing is there. That could explain it all — a defect of peripheral vision, a trick of my monkey mind, a flash of my confused and aging perception.

It is much better, though, to think that it follows me still, binding me to some far-off place where legions of men were beaten into namelessness by history. It must be better to think it is a strange and beautiful thing that is not concrete and cannot be explained. It is a demand for all things, good and bad, to happen, and for every thought to come to life. Places so literal cry out for the supernatural. There must be a dimension where fate and pity really do exist. There must be more. I insist on it.

ONE WHO DREAMS

REPRESENTING the Myanmar side was an official-looking man. There was no way to know what authority he had. He wore no uniform or identification, but he stood in the path of immigration with an interpreter who ushered us—no passport stamps required—to a waiting line of cars.

He was instantly wary of me. Whether the Thais notified them beforehand that an American would be coming, I do not know. I do not think I ever met the same Burmese person twice during the trip. They were constantly switched—maybe so we would not get to know them.

We were shown to a domestic flight. It was a normal internal flight commandeered by the military at the last moment for their purposes. The plane staff watched me with horror. It was as if they were seeing a polar bear boarding.

Then I arrived in old Mandalay.

Our motorcade zoomed by the precincts of the royal palace. Army barracks occupied the outskirts of the palace grounds, encircling it as if to emphasize military primacy over the unoccupied throne and the nation.

Not too many people got to Myanmar in those days, much less Mandalay. I wanted to think of the country as "Burma" — the nation's name before 1989. To one who washed up in Asia, "Burma" had an appealing old-fashioned ring to it — like "Siam" or "Formosa."

My method to enter the otherwise closed country was via an invitation from a Thai general to accompany a delegation on a special mission. A recently discovered ancient artifact was suspected to have belonged to a historical Thai hero. This top-secret discovery was connected to a centuries-past conflict between the kingdoms of Burma and Siam, mythologized with tales of royalty dueling on elephant back.

Investigation of the authenticity and powers of the artifact was a matter of national importance. An artifact that verified ancient myths could be used to strengthen ties, as well as afford magical protection to the no-doubt nefarious business deals being hatched between the nations. Importantly for both sides, it would be a good omen, omens being the most important ingredient for instilling confidence and peace of mind.

No matter the weight of the international sanctions on Myanmar at the time, Thailand and its neighbor were too close for any strictures made in cold far-off lands to separate them. Despite the historical propaganda that emphasized the enmity Thailand and Myanmar should have for each other, at a higher level, there was too long a border to be secured and too much money to be made for these ancient brother peoples to really hate. Hate was ok for the little people, but at a higher level it was bad for business.

I was invited on the trip due to my supposedly prophetic dream that revealed a curse on my boss's house. I can only speculate that the story had become magnified in its retelling, leading me to be called upon to observe certain incidents in certain situations—I cannot say more than that. My reputation caused me to be recommended for this trip. What I really was capable of, if anything, I myself did not know.

After my experience with the police empaths in Thailand, I knew that the role of the spirit world in the very highest reaches of the nation was usually hidden from foreigners. In an age of trendy hatred of religion and the denial of mythical rites, opinioned Westerners were unafraid even of death, separating themselves from the better part of all there was, scoffing at those who held indefensible beliefs.

While I too felt the desire to lecture Thai people on the civilized reality of the virgin birth over their old superstitions, I usually held my tongue. I wanted to feel their sincerity with no necessity to demand comparison or scientific proof. This world where every object could potentially become pure luck was a comfort. It let anyone reach out and grab the boon of fortune provided by belief.

I kept the details of the trip to myself at the office where I worked. Although Myanmar was not often on anyone's mind since the mass protests of 1988, it was a place that my government told me was bad and that I was wrong for visiting.

This was during the height of the sainthood that foreigners were heaping upon Aung San Suu Kyi. She was portrayed in the West as a Gandhi-like pacifist freedom fighter who was uniting the nation against its military overloads.

The type of Westerner I worked with in Bangkok was young and liberal, and I would surely be admonished for daring to go to a place that was repressive and had yet to live up to the standards of the rest of the world. I could not fault them for this viewpoint, but I had a bit of rebellion in me and it made me push against the wisdom of the day. I did not want to be part of anyone's rules. I wanted to see the tragedy of Burma with my own eyes.

The Burmese military was enveloped in mysticism, unparalleled at a national level in modern times. For example, in 1970, a ruling general dreamed that the side of the road the nation's cars drove on must be reversed in order to ensure good fortune. That very morning, the order was given and nationwide cars switched from driving on the left to driving on the right.

It became a nation of right-hand drive cars driving on the right side of the road. So, when overtaking, a driver had to poke the left side of his car out into the oncoming lane until it got out far enough for him, from his right-hand position, to see the road ahead. This unsafe situation led to many epic crashes over the years.

There was something mesmerizing about a world where edicts could come down from above and change the land overnight. It was something from the simplified universe of children's storybooks. In the real world it was frightening—a ruler's whim infecting the empire and decisions based on the phantoms of sleep.

I did not doubt there was a weight of oppression on the land via its dictatorship that had ruled in one form or another since 1962. Thailand relished its closed and backwards neighbor, as it was the source of endless resources and potential infrastructure projects. Its government was thought to be easily compromised by the sophisticated and bribe-laden Thais.

The Thai general confidentially explained to me that the Burmese were different than any other people and it took some level of continual cruelty to hover over them and beat them into shape. "There will never be a respite from this," he assured me matter-of-factly.

I was intrigued that someone of his importance was personally going on this trip as well. It meant what we were doing was a big deal.

The general was trained in modern techniques of military science in the United States (and at U.S. taxpayer expense), but entirely missed the ethics and morals that the Americans thought they were instilling by allowing him to be impressed by eating in their McDonalds and shopping at their Walmarts. He was cautious and serious, but arrived at one of the parties these men had, dancing like Jackie Gleason, light and happy, his formidable bulk sweeping this way and that. These parties could only be described as tribal, with groups of military men renewing their bonds each year and pledging mutual fealty to each other.

Also joining us was Pam, the top police empath, or what a Westerner would probably call a psychic. He was male, but feminine, the very embodiment of the Thai conceptualization of the in-between human. Like representations of the Buddha, he cultivated being neither fully male nor female. He was revered, even feared, by the other Thais for his supposed powers, but he spoke in an overconfident and flowery manner that betrayed to me his insecurity.

Mandalay was a stark contrast to the cities in other Asian Tiger nations at the time. It was not enveloped in a cloud of construction dust and its horizon was not a forest of construction cranes. Instead, the theme was sleepiness — no Western chain stores or skyscrapers as in neighboring Thailand, but instead, malaise in a state where the military monopolized economic power.

In coming years, at least 200,000 Chinese migrants would arrive and take over the city's commerce and transform it into a bustling Chinese-dominated city, but back then it was still a sleepy native town with sleepy businesses.

I ventured out into the streets on my own. It was quiet even during the day. A few stores had food and merchandise from China or Thailand, all in cheap-looking, utilitarian packaging.

The only bustle was at a market where fresh produce and meats were sold. It was all under low umbrellas that made every aisle of the market an enclosed passage in between tables laden with mounds of vegetables and meat being chopped into cuts before my eyes.

Those at the market gasped with surprise when they first saw me making my way through, partially bent over to avoid being poked by one of the rusty, protruding umbrella tines.

Not knowing the Burmese language and not being very good at Thai, I was generally isolated from both the Burmese and the Thai delegation I was traveling with. The Thais politely smiled, as they always did, but they would have done so anyway, pretending they could tolerate me even when they could not. The Burmese kept me at arm's length and made no attempt to engage me or even fearfully study me as some Thais did, viewing me sometimes as if they were beholding a dumb bear in a zoo that was oblivious to wide-eyed stares and hushed whispers. I was just invisible.

I pretended not to notice and did not make an effort to press myself on the Burmese. I had seen Westerners put on an overly friendly demeanor with Thais, never realizing the discomfort they caused, so I just tried to let the Burmese get used to me on their own terms.

As in Thailand, if the worst happened and I embarrassed myself or insulted someone, it would be written off as the incomprehensible act of a white person — an overly demonstrative race known for being impossible to figure out and not sensible in their impulses.

The general, while having invited me, also watched me closely. I had the impression he wanted to know if I possessed abilities or if I was faking it. Such skepticism would never be openly expressed even if it was shown I was an abject fraud, but I felt he was wondering what I would say about the artifact and if I was who I said I was.

I was on a precipice in a far-off land, one that was decades behind its nearest neighbors, in a pariah state that demanded what it did was legitimate. I was indulging myself in superstition, and sometimes, when I was not careful enough, really believed I was a seer. My education told me that just imagining such a thing meant I was a fool, but yet I knew I was not a fool. I knew what was real and what was not. All these alien people trusted me with magic things that logic told me must only be a reflection of something nestled deep in my own mind.

Our delegation stayed at a sterile state guest house — likely run by the military — but even there the electricity went off a few times. We participated in some sociable activities such as hitting golf balls at a military base. Each ball was painted gold and numbered.

We were presented with dinner and a traditional dancing show, but such traditional dancing only annoyed the Thais. Several nations in the region, including Cambodia, vied for the ownership of this traditional dance style, branding other nations as copycats who had stolen their traditions. I saw the stern look on the general's face as we watched the show and asked, "Do you like it?" and with a directness and fervor unusual for a Thai's typical way of indirect expression, he said, "I do not!"

The Burmese served wine which impressed the Thais. This was during one of the periodic wine crazes that gripped the region when wine suddenly became the hottest fad and people competed to show they consumed the most rarified vintages. I did not really appreciate it at the time, but these activities were the epitome of the Asian Tiger era — sipping expensive wine and hitting golden golf balls in one of the poorest regions in the world.

Many more men — undoubtedly military — attended the dinner. They glared at me with wide-eyed suspicion. I pretended I did not notice this and tried to be as unobtrusive as possible, quietly chatting with Pam.

"This wine is £1,000 a bottle in the U.K.," Pam informed me. Keeping the aura of a holy person, he did not usually drink in public. However, a £1,000 bottle of wine was too much for him and he was taking several long sips.

I never drank wine myself, but I succumbed to the bourgeois appeal as well and drank the expensive wine. I suppose it was good, but I was not knowledgeable enough to really know.

"So what were you doing in town?" Pam asked.

"How did you even know I went out?"

"They follow you everywhere, of course. They know where you go."

I pretended I was not surprised. "Something funny did happen," I said. "When I was waiting to cross a street, a young man pushed through the crowd and just shoved me out of the way with both hands. It was not only me, it was others too. No one got mad."

This was a weird occurrence. The young man had been wearing an old-fashioned wrap-around longyi, a type of sarong. After I was pushed out of the way, the immediate involuntary response was to confront or even punch him, but in the moment it was happening, it was so surprising that I just looked around to see if anyone else had reacted. No one had taken any notice.

"Yes, we know about this," Pam said. "These are, I think you would call in English, 'country people.' They have no etiquette yet and will push you because they have to go somewhere."

That made sense, I thought. This was their land and I was a strange thing only passing through.

"Lucky I didn't punch him," I said, obviously in jest.

"Yes, this is important," he said, referring to the propriety of our mission. He switched back to his customary water, setting his wine glass beside my plate as if no one would notice it was once his. He took a long drink of water. Putting down the glass he said, "I was surprised that you came along."

"It is exciting to be asked," I said, purposely ignoring the insult I thought he meant by his comment.

Pam reversed course as if to reassure me he was happy I was there. "The general is usually cautious, but after you speak with him, he is more aggressive in his activities. We know this is a once-in-a-lifetime opportunity to be in this position, so he has to make the most of it."

This was in reference to the boon of luck that was open to high officials. These people, by dint of their influence, would be invited to participate in, and sometimes force their way into, lucrative businesses and contracts. The best opportunities were open to those at the very top.

The general was either too cautious or honest, I never knew which. Pam and the other underlings were chafing at his reticence to indulge in these business activities fully. Doing so meant that money and positions on boards flowed down to those in his inner circle. Generals have to be completely confident to both succeed in military matters and also be corrupt. My general's reticence was seen as an unfortunate character flaw.

"Do you have any impressions so far?" Pam said, referring to the artifact.

"I don't know. I haven't even seen it yet," I replied.

He thought I was ducking the question. "Only someone with real abilities can tell something like this. These men were heroes. They were our heroes. You couldn't know!" He was almost shouting now, but the room was loud and no one noticed. I think he was a little drunk.

"It is authentic?" I asked, as if I completely agreed with everything he said.

"We will have to see what you think," he said. It was rare for a Thai not to be forthcoming with his expertise when asked. It revealed to me the pressure I was under to come up with revelations about the artifact as well as the resentment Pam felt towards me.

Even if it were possible to predict or sense something magical, surely sometimes there would be nothing to sense. At the same time, there was pressure to be bigger and better in one's predictions every time and even say what people demanded to hear. It made me realize the never-ending mix of expectation and self-delusion Pam subjected himself to — and that I must be sliding into as well.

Suddenly I realized that the general was speaking about me to the crowd in Thai. The interpreter then explained to the Burmese generals what had just been said in Thai to introduce me. This was to be my opportunity to ingratiate myself with the skeptical Burmese, but none of the Thais had told me anything beforehand. I guess they thought I knew this already. At least I did not have any time to worry. As so often, things just happened.

I knew what the general had alluded to in his speech. At a prior function in Thailand, just like this one, I told a folk tale that I made up and it went over well with the audience. I originally dreamed some of it and then embellished it a bit to make it seem more like a proper fable.

The average Thai had an expansive, even extraordinary knowledge of Aesop's Fables far beyond the handful of fables that a typical Westerner was familiar with.

Even at the highest levels of power, Thais were always known by their nicknames, for example *Nua* ("Mouse") or *Maew* ("Cat"). As Aesop's Fables had animals as the protagonists, these animals meshed nicely with the nicknames Thai preferred. Newspaper headlines, reporting on politicians, utilized their nicknames, stating things like "The Cat over the Lions" to express that a certain politician with the nickname of *Maew* ("Cat") was prevailing over political "lions" as in the style of a fable. I found out later that luckily the Burmese were just as steeped in Aesop's Fables as the Thais were.

I was trying to replicate the local receptiveness to Aesop's Fables with my own tale. My own fable originally had a monkey and a mule, but these morphed into something else outside of the realm of animals, but still hopefully keeping the flavor of Aesop's Fables.

The group was being told I was going to tell them a story.

I looked over at the general and he nodded his head as if to say, "Go ahead."

It was one of those singularly weird and uplifting times. I was far away and then even further on, deep in the forbidden land I could never understand, in this unusual company, for a supernatural mission.

As I began, one of the soldiers started interpreting it directly into Burmese. As with all interpretation, it gave the tale a halting quality at first as my English paused for the Burmese, but gradually it blended into a regular cadence as the two languages fell into a wave-like pattern.

The tale went something like this:

> *A Giant Wades Ashore*
>
> *A giant swam from a distant island — so far away one could not see the island, but that is where he said he came from. He waded ashore fully clothed. He shivered and shook like a dog, throwing off the water and almost drying himself.*
>
> *On the beach was a small restaurant. It was a ramshackle affair, but the cook, Khun Pom, was kind and sincere. People lined up all day to taste his food. The giant strode up to the restaurant owner and looked around.*
>
> *Khun Pom half-expected the giant to start breaking up his place, as giants were known to be strange, but he*

also thought that if the giant acted civilly, he might become a good customer.

The giant poured out gold coins of various sizes from a pouch onto a table and said, "What can I get for this?"

The shop owner could not fully contain his excitement, but tried to speak nonchalantly.

"What would you like?"

"Eggs," the giant said, salivating.

Khun Pom showed the giant to a table. Luckily, the chair at the table was made from a huge stump that just fit the giant.

Khun Pom gathered up the gold coins and counted them, giving some back to the giant.

"It only costs this much for 9 eggs. Is that enough?"

The giant was surprised, "Yes! I didn't expect change."

"We are only charging you what we would anyone else — for 9 eggs."

The giant was impressed. This showed Khun Pom was honest. Khun Pom could have taken more, as giants were easily fooled — still he would make a handy profit. The giant ate the eggs with gusto.

After that, the giant often returned and Khun Pom was glad to see him. Giants had plenty of money.

A lady farmer who Khun Pom bought eggs from at first could not understand why he now needed so many more.

"My customer is a giant," he said, stretching his hands to try to show the dimensions.

The farmer lady did not believe him, but she was glad to sell the eggs.

Of course, Khun Pom had a beautiful daughter. He did not know when it started, but soon realized the giant was flattering her, and she was clearly curious about him.

The giant brought Khun Pom's daughter a garland of strange plastic flowers that Khun Pom had never seen before. The neighbors were impressed as well.

Khun Pom knew she would be open to his charms, as her own late mother was fearless and confident. Khun Pom did not want her to marry a brute who would take her away to his unseen land in the ocean. And the giant did not understand Khun Pom's ways, once wearing his huge dirty sandals right into his house. He could not be a real husband for her.

So Khun Pom hatched a plan.

He cut back on the eggs he served the giant, but kept telling him it was 9. Hopefully the giant would get the message and find eggs to eat elsewhere.

However, the giant still flirted with his daughter and Khun Pom found he was making an even bigger profit by shortchanging the giant on eggs.

Finally, the giant walked along the beachside with his daughter in plain view of everyone. This was too much, even with the money the giant was spending in Khun Pom's restaurant.

The next day, the vendor served the giant one egg.

"This is it?" the giant asked.

"Yes, 9 eggs," Khun Pom said defiantly. He had to be brave now, he thought, smiling brightly.

The giant looked quizzically, then with a flash of anger, then quizzically again.

The giant said, "This isn't enough!"

"No," Khun Pom said, "9 eggs." He gave the giant his best sincere smile, one he had worked on his entire life.

"Should I pretend it is 9 eggs?" the giant thought. "Should I say something?" This did not seem real. Maybe he did not understand these people. The giant, confused, instead smashed the one egg he was served and walked out to sea, never to return to the restaurant again.

Khun Pom's daughter finally did go off to live with
another giant, but Khun Pom accepted it and proudly
served 9 eggs to any giant who ordered them.

This was the tale I told. Towards the end, I wondered how much time had passed, but the audience was wide-eyed with attention.

The Burmese generals started nodding and then clapped and laughed while drinking the expensive wine. This broke the ice. Whether this was in embarrassment for me or if they could draw out some meaning and thus believed I was a person who accepted them, I do not know.

The next day, I was to be escorted to see what had been found. It was me, the general, Pam and a few aides from the Thai side and a phalanx of Burmese military men. I knew both the general and Pam were watching me. I thought I detected the faintest squint of the eye from the general and I imagined he was wondering if I really could do this and what I might predict.

Pam's petulance had been at work. The elevator in the guest house broke down, stranding me on the fourth floor — there were no stairs to take or at least none that were unlocked and that I was able to access. I was stuck waiting for the elevator and was the last of the group to make it to the ground floor once the elevator was working. During that time, Pam had done his best to insinuate I had overslept and was causing everyone to wait. I only later realized this and at the time wondered why the general patted me on the back saying, "That's ok," with a smile, as if he was signaling that, in this generosity, he was excusing me for making him wait.

We were taken outside of town in a convoy to another military base. The general was driven in a shiny Mercedes and I was afforded the honor of sitting in the back with him. Perhaps it was another concession to me — making me know all was forgiven for making everyone wait. Pam had to sit in front, once quietly complaining about having to sit in the bright sunlight that shone through the front window onto him.

The military base surrounded a complex of old temples where official-looking guards stood at attention everywhere. The stone structures there, while made of reddish stone blocks, were well-maintained and complete. I later learned this was because the ancient stone buildings were constantly rebuilt and maintained, often with little regard to their original form, as they were living places still used to worship more or less the same gods as centuries ago. This constant remodeling was derided by foreigners, who thought that the insensitive modern changes slowly obliterated the temple's original form and cultural cues from earlier times.

The convoy stopped outside of a metal pole barn. Inside was a huge Buddha image that barely fit in the structure, flanked by neat piles of stones from the building that once covered it. The original stone structure probably could not be salvaged or was too big to be rebuilt and thus the entire area was covered by the modern metal building instead. Dark-red robed monks continually chanted the entire time we were there.

We paid our respects, kneeling before the massive Buddha image and holding incense, as was the custom. It loomed over us, seeming to lean forward, as we knelt there. It was a Burmese-style Buddha with a slightly square and broad face and extra-large eyes with heavy lids. This informed the Thais that, despite the friendship, the artifact's blessing would fall upon this land.

We exited the structure and passed an elaborate marionette show where large puppets performed to an empty audience. The show was going on 24 hours a day to honor the supposed spirits surrounding the artifact. Pam told me that the marionettes were specially imbued with human life for the performance and thus the marionette of the king and his ministers on the stage were channeling the actual spirits of men long dead. He said this as if it was his accomplishment. The show continued to its invisible audience and we continued on.

A short way later, we came to a knot of trees perched on a large pile of rubble from a collapsed structure. This was the only real ruin in the otherwise restored temple compound. Here there were guards as well, but in costume-like ancient garb, wearing Burmese-style battle helmets and holding ornamental staffs. These traditionally styled guards were huge men, the largest Burmese — or Thais, for that matter — that I had ever seen.

We climbed over the rubble to a clearing where six men stood around a massive stone slab. As we approached, they reached down and, in a single heave, violently slid back the slab with a bassy thump and then stood at attention again. Under where the slab had been was a wide and steep stair leading into the earth. I immediately smelled cool moist air wafting up.

Without stopping, our delegation descended the stairs. At the bottom was a long, low-ceilinged rectangular space that was made of ancient-looking stone blocks. Electric lights at the far end led us forward towards an altar.

On the altar was a massive oval platter and on that sat an elaborate wooden cradle which held the thing. It was less than a meter long and looked like a hunk of corrosion — in some places green and in others bluish. This was the legendary sword. It was composed of layers of rusted, flaking metal. Some flakes had fallen from it onto the platter.

The sword was said to make men tremble when they touched it and there were reports of those in contact with it being lucky in business and health. I knew that possession of such an item conferred destiny and legitimacy — something the ruling Myanmar military assumed of themselves and yet still craved.

Unbeknownst to me at the time, Pam had already examined the artifact. Later I learned it had manifested magical properties, as well as persistently entering the dreams of the very highest rulers of each of the lands. This was why a concerted effort was being made to understand its potential power and meaning. X-rays were taken of it and astrologers of the various ethnic groups that made up Myanmar were brought in to offer their own impressions.

I felt privileged as I stood before it, exposed to this hidden world. It might all be a scam by the crazy scoundrels who ran this police state made real by my own demand for the exotic, but I was there to receive the adventure. I had come to it somehow.

Belief in the power of this artifact was real. Thus it had a sort of actual power. It was the embrace of belief—all was real and was taken as such. It was the opposite of the Buddhist concept of emptiness, but close to the Thai Thereavada Buddhist imperative of fatalism—the accepting of fate and thus all there is. It must have been a vestige of the animism that preceded religion as well. It was when everything was real—the curses, the luck, the exacting consequences, good and bad—every action and every imagination. The very rocks had life.

Then, from behind the altar, a form slowly arose. It was only a head of sleek black hair, impossibly long and shiny, obscuring the body. It turned to us. It was a little girl dressed in what looked like a traditional Thai costume—a highly ornamented wrap-around silk garment. Her child's face was covered in heavy makeup to make her look like a glamorous adult. I did not have a chance to think, but caught my breath and tried not to show I was startled.

The girl had been lying on a mat behind the altar. In her mouth, she held a thick cigar-like cheroot. It smoldered as she regarded us with a haughty, worldly look. This was a young child who was provided as the ritual wife to the spirit that was thought to reside in the sword, accompanying it in the dark chamber day after day— a Thai whore for the sword. The Burmese with us smirked and the general was passively stoic—Thais at the highest levels being used to outrages for the good of the nation.

The still air grew electric. It was not clear if this creature was analyzing us or we were analyzing her—so many strange people in this place. Then a look of sudden boredom crossed her face and she slowly walked to the far end of the room. Our eyes followed her in unison. I wondered what indignities she must have experienced in this place and in this land. She flowed up the stairs without a word, disappearing from the chamber like a ghost.

I was beginning to realize that I was to stay in the chamber for the night. This may have been explained to me in Thai at some point earlier and it had been assumed I understood. As this was going through my mind, the men turned and headed back to the chamber's exit. I again pretended that I was not surprised.

I was expected to dream. I was not told what I was expected to dream about, but I knew that the desire was to know about the authenticity of the thing. It was the common man's assumption of archeology—find a corroded sword, then it obviously must come from a king, not from the legions of foot soldiers who were far more numerous and must have died in greater numbers, leaving plenty of common swords.

There was a bedroll set off to one side of the chamber for me. Along with it were the typical implements of sleep—talcum powder, a towel, and a longyi. Also provided were a few cans of Coke, a plastic ice bucket, bottles of water and a package of crisps.

There were smiles and Thai-style *wais* all around to me. The general looked hopeful and Pam forced a smile, as if he thought I was unable to detect his ill-will. The men exited up the stairs and the slab slid back into place, making an incredibly resonant scraping sound as it moved. Then I was alone.

I was good at spinning worst-case scenarios in my mind. I wondered, "What if an army truck was parked nearby and left idling and carbon monoxide leaked down into the chamber, suffocating me?" Potentially more alarming was the apparent lack of a bathroom, but I found several large trash buckets by the stairway that would probably suffice. I decided to look for any cameras, thinking they must be observing me, but did not find any. I did find the switch for the lights by the stairs, so I could turn them on and off at will.

I unrolled the bedroll and sat in the silence. I ate the package of crisps. Sounds were deadened in the enclosed chamber and every crunch of my eating the crisps sounded like it was coming from inside my head.

Without warning, the lights went out. I felt my way to the light switch, but it no longer worked. I decided to sleep. I was sent here to dream, so that is what I would try to do.

I kept waking up again and again. In the complete silence, I think I might have been awakened by my own snoring echoing off the walls. I was entombed in rock, sleeping on a hard floor, and my bladder was becoming uncomfortably full. I rolled over and tried to dream.

Sometime in the night I awoke and stayed awake. I got up and approached the altar.

I did not want to leave without holding this sword myself. I once more glanced around for cameras, as I did not know if I was allowed to touch it. I saw nothing. I grasped the sword at either end and carefully lifted it. It was not heavy. It was clearly a corroded hunk of something, but it was hard to tell what it really was.

It was then that my eyes rested on one of the lights that flanked the altar. It was not on. Then I looked to the other. It was not on either. The chamber should have been pitch dark, but instead there was a cold diffuse light surrounding the altar. It was nearly shadowless, and, as I held the sword close to my eyes, I thought, "Is it glowing?"

I was certain I was awake. I checked to see if there were cracks in the walls or ceiling that could be allowing outside light to enter. There was nothing. I could not see where the light was coming from and yet the chamber was illuminated. It was almost not surprising in this place.

Clutching the sword with both hands, I found myself involuntarily pressing it against my chest as I looked around for the source of light. I wondered what foot soldier or king wielded the sword — or if it was a sword at all. I wondered why a magic thing would really exist in this repressive state. I wondered what confluence of events in ancient days imbued it with magic or at least the power to move men to wonder at it and covet it all these years later.

I carefully put it back, making sure to set it in the same way so it could not be determined that I had handled it. I lay down again, several times opening my eyes to view the altar. It was as still as ever.

Despite the frisson of adventure and exoticism that I had exposed myself to, I knew. Away from the wine dinners and golf courses and artifacts were the cruel and condescending rule and the endless hidden ulterior motives of military clans.

The next thing I remember was the sound of the stone cover being pushed away. I felt that I had experienced a deep and timeless sleep.

I scrambled up and stood on the stairs just in time to see the expectant faces of the anonymous Burmese and Pam and the general. I felt pressure to tell them something momentous, but they were suddenly right there in front of me.

Had I been savvier, I might have built my reputation, making it appear as if I was truly a prescient person. I knew how to say things they would have believed and that would have seemed completely true from their perspective. In this region, that meant powerful friends and money. But I was not quick enough or greedy enough. I was too naive to take the advantage. I did not know what to say, so I just decided to tell the truth. I told them I did not dream that night. The sword had said nothing to me.

They were clearly disappointed and even Pam appeared shocked. The general was stony-faced, perhaps a bit angry.

After exiting the chamber, I was led to soldiers at a table with paperwork. They patted me down rather roughly and had me empty my pockets. Pam told me they were checking for flakes stolen from the artifact that could be incorporated into the amulets that people customarily wore.

As this was happening, I began to remember that I did dream — I was now certain of it — but I could not recall the dream. It was flitting away as I was exposed to the sunlight and the reality of the day.

The marionettes were still flailing and dancing like pretend humans as we exited the compound.

Once we got back into the convoy of vehicles, I suddenly thought to say to the general, "There was a glow around the sword."

He replied, almost with annoyance, "They know that."

I had not played along. Not dreaming was pointing out the absurdity of the situation and causing uncertainty.

As we drove back, Pam was seated in the back, speaking to the general energetically in Thai, emphasizing his impressions and that further arcane ceremonies needed to be performed.

As Thais tended to value all in a group being of the same positive mind, the general leaned forward and touched me on the shoulder saying, "It's ok. It's ok."

Then Pam spoke to the general again, but this time in English, as if to ensure I was included.

"This is an omen—a good omen. There is nothing stopping you."

GOING TO THE SOUTH

IT was silent in the car as it often was. My wife played the same songs over and over on the car's cassette player, songs that we had once both liked.

The time we first met was from another decade, with its fashion and music already passing into quaintness. The music on the cassette was from that time. The catchy and romantic songs we once listened to together were the sound of our nostalgia. I could not stand them anymore, but I said nothing.

We played the cassette all the way through several times, as it was an all-day drive from Bangkok to Songkhla Province in the Thai south on the Malay Peninsula. We were going back to my wife's hometown to help her father, who was retiring from the police force.

He was one of those ultra-lean and dark men of the tropics, who moved slowly but surely in the intense heat of his world, never seeming to sweat. Quiet, with suspicious eyes. You had to accept him before he accepted you.

In recent years he had become ill and even leaner, as if his muscles were tightening around his bones. The reasons were vague — drinking — a natural reason, as the police officers were offered free drinks wherever then went. Then there was apparently tuberculosis. I wondered if it might be something worse.

We visited him in the police ward of the government hospital. Men lay in a line of beds in the ward, having placed their police hats at their bedsides to indicate their rank to the others. Most were scrawny and painfully skinny. Liver problems, both from drinking and from infection from liver flukes, were a common ailment.

I *waied* my father-in-law. The *wai* is the Thai gesture of greeting and respect created by placing the hands together in front of the face for a moment as if in prayer. I had been told I had a beautiful *wai* and I always followed correct etiquette in greeting, but beyond that, we did not have much to say to each other. I was strangely reticent around in-laws. It should have been enough that I was there with them, I thought.

He had once showed me around a sprawling fish market in town. It was interesting and I attempted to look impressed, but did not know what to say. I probably was not the son-in-law he envisioned. I was a blank cipher, an alien who could never really connect with him or tune in to the same things a Thai cop would be inclined to be concerned about in his seaside town. I was not the expected thing.

My wife spoke and then argued with him a bit as she usually did. She had proudly purchased an expensive insurance policy that would have put him in a private room in a private hospital, but he would have none of it. He wanted to be in this basic ward reserved for police officers. Each day he swapped stories with the other dying men. This was the camaraderie and honor he expected.

She was annoyed with this, as she had a young person's direct way of wanting to do things that the slow older folks of the countryside just scoffed at. Beyond this vague understanding, I had little idea what was being said. The dialect of Thai language spoken in the south was different than that spoken in Bangkok, with hard accented consonants and a generally more rapid cadence, so that it sounded as if the speaker was about to burst into anger.

It was assumed that the end was coming for her father, so it was decided — in those harsh southern tones — that we would drive to his police station to pack up his belongings. The station was located farther south in what was once part of the ancient Pattani Sultanate, a small doomed kingdom that was wedged in between Siam and modern-day Malaysia to the south. It was predominately Muslim and had its own language and Arabic script for writing.

We hurried away from the hospital. I felt impatient for some reason, and she did too. It was the one thing we felt together by then.

As we got into the car, I asked, "Do you want to drive by the beach?"

"No," she sniffed.

Very well, I thought to myself, we will go directly to the police station. I was not going to say anything more. I do not know why this seemed to be the proper response. I think I believed that it was admirable to avoid conflict and especially bad feelings at all costs. Only many years later did I realize we never talked about anything important and thus never got past the slights of each day. We wasted our time.

After I was first married, I vividly dreamed that I realized it was another woman who I really loved instead. Only after I awoke did I realize that the woman I dreamed of was the idealized version of my wife I imagined when we first met. The dream only added to my hurt feelings, as if she was somehow to blame for becoming a real person in my eyes. It was the foolishness of a young man who could not reconcile the dream and reality of women and what he wanted them to be.

The land we were passing through was idyllic, with groves of palm trees by the ocean trembling in the otherwise still air. Rolling green hills sometimes reared up unexpectedly to sharp mountains with exposed outcroppings of weathered grey and black rock. The harsh sun illuminated every color, every green of the leaves. The brown of the dirt roads was like seeing a world that could not be spoiled.

It was immediately apparent when one passed from the Buddhist-dominated north of the province to the Muslim south where we were headed. In the north, fishing vessels moored anywhere they wanted and the beaches were strewn with fishing nets, broken Styrofoam and beer bottles. The Muslim south, though poorer, was more orderly. Boats landed only in designated areas and the beaches were largely free of the carefree debris of the Buddhist north.

Every bit of arable interior land had been converted to rubber plantations. The rubber trees marched in a uniform grid unchecked across every hill and vale. Once a teeming jungle, there was now only hard-packed dirt where rubber tappers drove their motorcycles to tap the trees.

During the Cold War, this was the land of communists and bandits who found hiding places among the many rough mountaintops and caves and benefitted by being able to slip over the porous border into Malaysia.

By the 1990s, communism had faded away and the Thai army had managed to subdue the separatist movement in the southernmost provinces, monopolizing both a network of informants that allowed authorities to prevent violence, as well as the bribes that enriched those in charge and pacified the lowly. The military met troublemakers with unspeakable repression and torture while accepting the local "foreign" Pattani culture as being equal and part of the dominant Buddhist Thai nation. This situation, meted out by the military, provided peace, but left the police as unconnected and impoverished bureaucrats pining for the day when the military would be stripped of their authority in the south and the police would be back in charge.

At the turn of the century, just such an eventuality occurred. With the military removed from administering the Deep South provinces, the police liquidated the network of informants and upped the bribes on criminal activity, thus alienating the populace, and the "restive Thai south" (as newspapers around the world began to refer to it) erupted again into a bloody low-grade insurgency.

As we rode along that day, at the end of the Cold War and before the era of radical Islamists, the Thai Deep South was peaceful. The call to prayer at the city mosque was reassuring and added to the harmonious quality of cities by the sea and waving palm trees.

My father-in-law's police station was typical of those lazy peaceful times. It contained an aquarium, as was once popular with Thai police. Its fish were doted on by the officers, along with stray dogs and cats and uncounted potted plants both inside and out. The building had gaping holes in the walls where plaster had fallen away from the wooden framework. This left only a skeleton-like structure of dark grey sun-baked wood instead of walls. From inside any room, one could see through the walls to the greenery outside. The roof looked sturdy, but had been patched many times, no doubt by the officers of the station themselves, when leaks started. The station was an oddly comfortable and cheery place, as if it were a derelict building that children had converted for their own use.

In contrast, the military in the region operated out of extensive and orderly bases with largely modern equipment. Thailand's regular coups ensured that military-led governments periodically topped up spending on their own forces. The time had long passed when the lowly police could muster any political pressure to improve their own equipment and surroundings.

The walls of the holding cell in the police station were only horizontal wooden slats through which one could see to the outside. A rope was strung across the opening where a door would have been to remind those placed inside that they were honor-bound to respect the dimensions of the room and not escape.

No one was in the cell that day. I suspected that the military would take away any real troublemakers, leaving the police to the petty criminals or drunkards who could be shamed into staying behind the rope.

My wife and I, in a silent and businesslike way, gathered up my father-in-law's belongings, which included clean threadbare uniforms and various insignia denoting his rank and years of tenure.

We could have reflected on the sadness of what we were doing — clearing up the loose ends of her father's life — but we did not think to pause. At least, I did not. I kept my mind firmly on what I was doing and neither of us spoke.

Most striking was my father-in-law's fragile gun. It was missing the chamber part and was in two pieces that barely held together. This was not unusual, as the underfunded police needed to take out personal loans if they wanted working modern equipment. The state of this gun also indicated the peace and relative level of crime that was dealt with then.

In a moment which I knew even then I would long remember, I held the gun in both of my hands, and the two pieces started to pivot apart, nearly splitting the gun in two, but I was just able to hold it together. Forever after that, I would sometimes have dreams in which I was under attack. In the dream I would reach for a gun and it was always that broken one. I would have to cradle it in both hands to keep it from falling apart.

After leaving the police station, my wife and I visited an aunt or family friend. I could not pin down whether the lady was actually part of the family or just an honorary family member, as was often the case with close family acquaintances in Thailand.

The lady we were meeting was a one-eyed, toothless, missing-toed grandma; however, she was not some coarse country person, but a dignified lady who just did not care to have teeth anymore.

She was large and walked with a bow-legged waddle, but everything about her manner expressed her strength. On the walls of her house were photos of her and her friends in their youth, and one could see who would die first. The rail-thin, delicate, sexy ladies were all long gone. Auntie had waddled to their funerals solid as a truck. She would be one of the lucky ones, living out her days in perfect health until the end, when one morning she would not wake up.

Her home had impressive expanses of marble flooring. Her daughter, also prematurely dead from some female ailment, had insisted on high-class marble and a proper dining room with a grand table and high-back chairs, none of which were ever used. Auntie preferred eating the traditional way, sitting on the floor with an array of dishes laid out on a straw mat.

That day, Auntie sat on the edge of her shiny wooden teak bed ("Soft mattresses are bad for you," she advised) and regarded me with a smile that was not a smile she put on like so many Thais, but simply part of her normal, placid expression. The whole room was made of that teak — cool and giving.

I was shocked when she began to speak to me in serviceable English.

"I graduated from Sarah Lawrence College," she said. "I was only one of two Thai people there." She quickly moved past these descriptive pleasantries. "You've come a long way to be here."

"Yes," I said. I realized she was asking me why.

I had come so far. I had come to the most exotic country I could think of, but that was not enough. From Bangkok I had traveled further — out into the provinces to this village, to find myself sitting before a graduate of Sarah Lawrence College.

"I've been far away on the other side of the world," she started, correctly assuming I had no explanation for my presence. "Everybody does things for their own reasons. It's no wonder there are wars!" she said with guttural chuckle. "Every day that goes by without a war is shocking. Everyone should get along, but they won't. It's not possible."

There was further talk in their southern-accented harsh-toned Thai, and at some point my wife said, "My husband drinks." Auntie looked right through me and my drunkenness. It was humiliating Thai pity. It was supposed to be a pleasure and an honor to receive it, and, at the same time, I knew that my wife's statement of fact, out loud, was a plea, a genuine plea that I could not dismiss or address.

Auntie reached under the bed and pulled out a wad of paper held together with string. It was bank books, deeds and various photos. She once owned land along the main road into town and slowly sold it off over the years—sending her kids to college, investing in stocks, growing aplenty.

"Look at these things," she said.

She handed me postcard-like images of old revered monks. Just seeing them was supposed to cure me. I looked at them. It was getting darker, and crickets chirped in the distant background, and every now and then, frogs chimed in with discordant croaks.

When Auntie was young, she went topless, as was the custom for older women in her day. After her granddaughters started attending university in Bangkok, they returned to modernize their grandmother, covering her bare breasts and explaining that women cover their breasts. The grandmother passively complied, but refused to speak about the past when her granddaughters reminisced about the days when their grandmother hilariously sat bare-breasted. She would only mutter, "Not fair."

It was dark by now. "We have to go," my wife said. I said nothing, as usual, and we departed.

I often recalled those monks on the postcards that Auntie showed me when I struggled with myself. Another world, another species. I wondered if they imagined a strange thing like me would one day be regarding their yellowing postcard faces. I thought all of this should have been easy. It should have worked.

We drove back along a road that paralleled, in various places, an old train track. It was once a narrow-gauge steam railway, built to transport produce from the various plantations to a wharf in the town of Songkhla.

Railroads fascinated me and this one in particular, with its kilometers of rail lines overtaken by encroaching buildings and roads, fascinated me even more. It was a broken thing, and I had walked the length of the track in the past, over rusty trestles and through tall stands of violently strong weeds that had attempted to stop me.

My wife once recounted that when she was a child, she rode the train to school in a passenger car that was added to bring people to and from nearby Hat Yai. At that time, the railway, the last steam train in Thailand, was in its final years of operation. The train was undependable and rickety, and, at one stretch up a gentle hill, she and the other passengers had to get out and walk alongside the train as it struggled to make it up the slightly inclined grade.

It was a life so different from mine, but we were drawn together and it had come to this.

Now my wife and I rushed by the railroad on a modern highway, with her father's uniforms, lunch pail, and broken revolver in a box in the back seat. It was quiet in the car until she turned on the radio and our cassette began again.

I knew everything about her and I was never closer to anyone, but we only seethed. Originally it was for some good reason, which I had forgotten. Now it was only out of foul habit.

BLACK MAY

I.

It was another day in my workaday life—putting on my dress slacks, Pierre Cardin belt and white shirt and walking to and from work with my little briefcase of papers. I cannot recall now what was so important that I had to carry those papers around each day. I think it was the daily newspaper, then one of the few connections to the wider world.

The only other overseas communication was via long-distance phones sitting on small stands in front of guest houses on Khao San Road, or letters that sometimes took three weeks to get back to the U.S.

Thailand was a place where one, newly arrived, could not read the language or even sound it out. Overheard conversations were as meaningless as the birds chirping. It allowed me to compress down, as in a vice, the scope of the world. I felt secure, nestled into one of a million concrete neighborhoods on the Siamese plains.

The spectacle of the exotic and the Buddhist and the royal conspired to give the impression of wide-open opportunity for discovery against an ancient backdrop. It was a distraction of endless baubles and flights of fancy to explore. Nothing was as it should be, but everything was exactly right.

The universe will not let any person feel secure — much less a young man who is built to go out and fight for a place in the world. I had just returned to Thailand from a week in Los Angeles where the Rodney King riots had burned through the city and right down the street where I had stayed with some friends on my trip. The next-door neighbors, angered by the verdict of not guilty in a police brutality case, expressed their ire by stealing televisions and sofas from nearby stores. This style of protest was repeated throughout Los Angeles, with buildings looted and then set ablaze in widespread opportunistic public anger.

I was stunned to see military Humvees on the streets of Los Angeles and hundreds of burned-out buildings. As an American of my day, cocooned in a soft, inward-looking nation, I considered civil unrest and military deployment something that happened in other nations, not my own.

Now I was back in Bangkok, where massive demonstrations sprawled out on the streets not far from where I lived. I had not been following events in Thailand while I was in the U.S., and this chaos that greeted me upon my return to the city took me by surprise. Censorship was in effect, but most newspapers published as usual. The *Bangkok Post* bowed to the ban, but was published with areas of white space where the banned news would have been. For some reason, this was praised as a sign of courage.

After days of ebb and flow in the protesters' locations, tens of thousands walked down Ratchadamnoen Avenue from Sanam Luang on a typically hot afternoon, apparently on their way to the parliament building.

Troops arrived and set up barbed wire at strategic bridges that led out of the area to bar the march of the protesters. This was well before many improvements were made in Bangkok transport. Most movement around the city was via narrow streets then — so this blockage by the military was significant.

Bangkok's Ratchadamnoen Avenue was designed to mimic Paris's Champs-Élysées and its wide, palatial expanses, crowned by Democracy Monument at its mid-point. It had long been a place where protests took place and blood was shed.

II.

THE genesis of what was happening in Thailand read like a quaint Cold War-era story, with military men in a developing country fearing they might soon be sacked. Eager to hold power uncontested, they conducted a coup, citing a number of pretexts.

On February 23, 1991, the Thai military, led by Sunthorn Kongsompong, staged a bloodless coup and installed a group of generals which named itself the National Peacekeeping Council. The constitution was abolished and martial law imposed. The coup was cleverly conducted under the cover of the first days of the Gulf War invasion. Thus, in the international press, news of the coup was buried by the attention-grabbing invasion of Iraq.

As the coup transpired, television channels were commandeered by the military and all showed the army TV station logo. Occasionally a recording was shown of a person, surrounded by menacing army personnel, reading a statement admitting he was involved in an assassination conspiracy. This was one of the reasons the generals said they needed to seize power.

The Chatichai Choonhavan-led government that was overthrown was notable as being part of the first peaceful changeover of power from one democratically elected government to another in Thailand when it took over from Prime Minister Prem Tinsulanonda. Together the Prem and Chatichai governments were largely responsible for setting the stage for Thailand's economic miracle of the 1980s and 1990s.

There was not much popular dissent against the coup at the time. The Chatichai government was perceived as corrupt and the Thai experiment with democracy was very young. Strong- arm rule was the norm in the past, with coups being the punctuation marks of brief Thai democratic experiments.

After the coup, disruption to everyday life was brief. A popular and credible interim prime minister — Anand Panyarachun — was installed by the military. As a former Thai ambassador to Canada, the U.S. and the U.N., he was well-known internationally. Besides the veneer of respectability he gave the regime, his tenure as prime minister would be notable for allowing awareness of HIV prevention to be widely disseminated for the first time.

Cracking down on unions was also a priority of the new regime. State labor unions were abolished, and one of the more notable excesses was the unexplained disappearance of labor activist Thanong Po-an.

New elections were held in May 1992. Despite their initial acquiesce to the coup, the public began to label political parties "good" or "evil," depending on which rushed to support the coup generals' continued power in government.

After the elections, events culminated in one of the coup generals, Suchinda Kraprayoon, being appointed prime minister. The opposition kept pressure on the government to appoint an elected person to be prime minister instead, and cited previous promises from Suchinda himself that he would not take the prime minister's post and continue the coup generals' domination of government.

A series of demonstrations against the government started and was centered around Sanam Luang, a large historic park in the old quarter of the city. Eventually the protests attracted more and more people and came to be called the "mobile phone mob," to refer to the newly affluent city dwellers with mobile phones that were flocking to oppose military rule.

This was the situation I was returning to.

III.

THE day after I returned to Bangkok, the bridge over the canal on Samsen Road near where I was living was sealed off. Mounds of barbed wire were unfurled, but some foot traffic was allowed to pass through. Other footbridges on the canal were left open. This bridge was a back exit for protesters on Ratchadamnoen Avenue to flee in the event of a crackdown. The barbed wire was a sign that the military was serious about putting pressure on those who had the temerity to call for elected leaders. At the same time, it left an outlet for protesters who had second thoughts and decided to leave.

Angry residents besieged troops at the barricades on the bridge by lining up dozens of motorcycles and blowing exhaust at the troops. Hundreds of men materialized on the military side, armed with bamboo riot shields. They looked around uncomfortably. Through the smoky exhaust haze, I saw the men were very young — possibly new recruits.

Throughout the protests, the military would be beset by hit and run motorcyclists with bandanas over their faces. They would roar up to military positions, blow exhaust or hurl items at the troops and then speed off.

In an unusual parallel to the riots in Los Angeles earlier in the month, it was later disclosed that no Thai government organization had much in way of a plan or equipment to deal with civil unrest. In Los Angeles, this resulted in the government being paralyzed and doing nothing. In Bangkok, it resulted in shooting at demonstrators.

Later in the night, both the protesters and the soldiers at the Samsen Road bridge spontaneously dispersed. The next morning, the barbed wire was pulled back and traffic returned to normal, as if to say, "We are all tired. Go home and we will try again tomorrow." That day's work and commerce then commenced as normal. Thais rarely let dirty political things interfere with daily living. ATMs always worked during coups and protests.

I walked to work in the morning, as usual. It was another hot and dry day, as nearly every day was in this city, but today the traffic, restricted by the military and protest presence, was greatly reduced. Walking to work took me over the formerly blocked bridge and then across Ratchadamnoen Avenue. Thousands of protesters were asleep or just beginning to stir along the road.

Phan Fa Bridge was at the head of the protest site on Ratchadamnoen Avenue. The military had blocked the bridge with barbed wire so the protesters could not reach parliament. Beyond the barbed wire was an endless sea of military men, sitting and resting in the last shade of the morning.

In those days, Thailand was rarely mentioned in the international media unless it was in connection with monkeys, elephants, or, especially in the British press, prostitution. While Thais tolerated or even embraced prostitution, they did not tolerate outsiders commenting on it.

Yet it was also a time when CNN influence and its worldwide reach was at its peak. In the previous year, CNN became the sole way to follow the action of the first Gulf War in real time. There was hope among the protesters that events on the streets in Bangkok might be able to play out live around the world.

To capitalize on this, the protesters, normally ensconced in their own insular language, made signs in English, French and German to cater to the foreign journalists presumed to be covering the events. Graffiti in English read "Suchinda Dictator" to point out how a coup general was assuming the post of prime minister even after elections. I never saw any foreign press, though.

I continued through the protesters, who were just rousing themselves as if to start their job of protesting for another day. I crossed Ratchadamnoen Avenue over to Sao Ching Cha — a part of the city studded with shops that made items related to Buddhist worship. Huge golden Buddhas for sale sat on the sidewalks.

That was where my office was, in one of nondescript concrete shophouses that lined the streets. Most of these were four stories high and could house virtually any type of business — Buddha shop, restaurant, mechanics shop, printing house, school, or just a residence. An ancient wooden home sometimes peeked out from between the concrete structures. They were the remnants of the original neighborhood, slowly supplanted by the shophouses over time. They sat directly behind the streetside shophouses that were built in their front yards to fully utilize the space.

Once at work, I was beginning to feel uneasy with what might occur in the political standoff happening all around me. This was not the civility and smiles that was advertised. It made the constant harangue about the friendliness of Thailand and the incessant grins that greeted me every day appear to be a ruse.

The school I worked at was a prep school for those wanting to study in overseas universities. The students were wealthier than average and from connected families. Not far from the school was the Defense Ministry, the Supreme Court, and the city government building, along with other important government and military facilities. The well-heeled students, trickling in and out of the school, made the place a hub for all manner of intelligence and gossip about the highest-level goings on in Thailand.

This meant that the results of Supreme Court decisions were known during school hours before they were released to the press. I was also privy to exactly when and how governments were reshuffled. Eventually, I realized that there were no secrets in Thailand. Telling someone, "This is a secret" only sped along the passage of information.

So that day at work, rumors circulated that the military was moving in many more troops. The troops were from upcountry and were receiving indoctrination that the protesters were communists, intent on revolution. This was supposedly a page out of Maoist battle theory. If locally based troops who knew the situation on the ground could not be trusted to fire on people, then bring in troops from far-off provinces and tell them the protesters were evil and thus could be shot.

The implications of this information were spontaneously understood and the school began to clear out. The street-level shops had shutters that were locked each night. I started hearing the shriek of metal shutters being pulled down all along the street and this indicated the common feeling that some conflagration was at hand.

By 1 p.m. most people had left the school. I was lost in something I was doing and it suddenly struck me that I should leave as well. If anything bad happened on Ratchadamnoen Avenue, it would prevent my return, as I needed to cross the road to get back to my room.

I left work and walked back to Ratchadamnoen Avenue. It was a blazing hot afternoon. Great sheets of plastic webbing were stretched across the avenue to provide shade to the crowds. Thousands camped along the street, mainly clumped into areas where they could get out of the sun. It was completely peaceful.

At the front lines, probably 10,000-15,000 protesters were camped out in front of Phan Fa Bridge. The bridge was blocked off with a mountain of barbed wire. The bridge has since been widened, but on that day it was a narrow choke point between the protesters and the road to parliament beyond. Trees around Phan Fa Bridge had men in them who appeared to be lookouts or possibly snipers. Beyond the bridge and barbed wire, the street split into several radial boulevards, and down each of these was a sea of soldiers and their vehicles, no doubt arranged to convince the protesters that they were vastly outnumbered and outgunned.

I decided to not return to my room, but remain with the protesters for a while. I had a vague notion that I wanted to see what would happen with my own eyes. Something terrible was about to become reality. If no one else could see it, at least I wanted to. The way I was walking around like an invisible man gave me the impression that I would be immune from anything that might occur.

Around the protest site I never saw any other foreigners or international media or satellite trucks. The country's TV and radio stations were controlled by the military and were playing patriotic music.

At a small gap in the barbed wire at the bridge I attempted to pass through, just to see if I could, but the soldiers would not let me pass. This was something different, as previously I could go anywhere I wished.

Several sour-faced characters were moving among the protesters and taking close-up photos of people in what appeared to be an attempt to intimidate. Whoever these people were, they have a photo of me. The man did not like it when I took his picture though. I am not sure why the protesters tolerated his presence. In spite of this, the atmosphere was relaxed, with little sign of worry or anxiousness.

One of the protest leaders, Chumlong Sirmuang, head of the Palang Dharma Party, was standing on a truck among the protesters. When I got up close and photographed him, he was one of the few people who seemed to notice me. At first he looked suspiciously and then gave me an uncertain smile and nod from his perch on top of the truck.

IV.

AS the afternoon wore on, more protesters retreated to the shade to rest. At Democracy Monument, people handed out rambutan, a juicy fruit, to refresh the crowd.

Suddenly, a line of soldiers formed at Kok Wua intersection. This was the opposite end of the street from Phan Fa Bridge. Democracy Monument was in between. This action was apparently to prevent protesters from escaping. They were going to be taught a lesson. Now they were boxed in and would have to make a last stand, ironically around Democracy Monument.

I had no idea of the timing of what might happen. Nor did I realize how ominous the military threat really was. The people and the soldiers were pleasant and well behaved. I was in Thailand, the land of smiles. I finally told myself it was too hot. Maybe it was an instinct to get out of the way, but I decided the heat was too much and that I should retreat back towards my room.

Within 10 minutes after I had left Ratchadamnoen Avenue, soldiers opened fire on the protesters to clear the street and arrest the protest leaders. I had just crossed a footbridge over Banglampoo Canal when I heard echoes of gunfire coming along the waterway.

I immediately ran back towards the commotion—back to Phra Sumen Road by Wat Bowonniwet, a temple. People were looking around curiously as I think most were still not convinced that the army would use live ammunition on people. Protesters started trickling in from the Phra Sumen-Dinso intersection, some limping and others being carried.

Then a phalanx of soldiers swung around the corner and looked down the street to where I was standing along with about 50 other people. They hesitated for a moment as if they were looking for something in the crowd. Then it was as if a decision was hastily made, and, in an instant, they leveled their guns and began firing at us. I was never sure what they were looking for. It could have been people taking photos, troublemaking motorcyclists, or maybe it was just an attempt to discipline the populace.

Everyone retreated. A few people fell and a handful were hit by gunfire or perhaps less-lethal buckshot.

After the first volley, the soldiers retreated back around the corner out of sight. An even bigger crowd amassed as a wounded motorcyclist and others were being helped up. People crowded around injured persons and piled them into the back of a car. As the car sped off, some of the people were shrieking with grief and anger at the soldiers. While I had imagined I was set apart from the increasing violence, I realized that my hands were shaking so much that I had to hold my camera against a telephone pole to keep it steady.

There was still much brave defiance left in the people. Incredibly, the crowd, including myself, drifted back down Phra Sumen Road towards where the shooting had taken place. We reached the end of an ancient wall that had once protected the city from invasion. The rest of the wall had been truncated and dismantled long ago so that ugly shophouses could occupy the space where the wall once stood.

Everyone was looking down the street, but I happened to look up and notice a soldier on the wall above us. He appeared to light a firecracker. I raised my camera to photograph him, but he raised his gun at me just as the firecrackers went off. So I fled with everyone else who thought the resulting noise was gunfire. There was controversy over the years as to whether soldiers used any warning before shooting into the crowds. During this incident, at least, I did witness some sort of firecracker being used to simulate the sound of gunfire and scare people away.

Once the noise had died down, the crowd quickly gravitated back to the end of the city wall again. Suddenly, there was a short, sharp retort of gunfire. It was so quick people did not have a chance to run, but after a moment, the crowd retreated a few steps and then stopped in confusion.

Fallen bodies were all around me.

Then the following happened in about 10 seconds: I noticed that a person who was standing about two meters from me had been shot in the head. Other people were crumpled in the street and little spatters of blood were everywhere. The wounded were beginning to be dragged away. Sobbing people surrounded me and told me how sorry they were. I pushed away from them to see a foreigner fatally shot and lying on the ground. By now my hands were shaking uncontrollably. I raised my camera over the heads of the furious crowd to try to photograph the dead man, who was now completely out of sight as people hunched over him. As I did so, I saw motion above me. I looked up and saw dozens of soldiers crowded onto the city wall. I just remember the details of one soldier — the one nearest to me who was drawing his rifle to aim at me. I do not know what anyone else was thinking, but all at once everyone drew a collective breath because they knew what was going to happen next — utter chaos breaking loose.

Bullets flew everywhere and this time it was sustained. I heard them whizzing to either side of me. The entire crowd, acting on instinct, turned in military-like unison and ran in the opposite direction. People stepped on each other's feet and ran right out of their shoes. I do not know if the people who fell around me were shot or just tripped, but no one looked back. Cement shards blew off the buildings and bullets impacted the street in front of me as I ran. The terrifying sounds of the shooting were probably amplified by the way the street was lined, typical Bangkok fashion, with cement walls and buildings. I did manage to take one photo (the last on the roll of film) as I continued to run. It just captured people running and smoke in the street.

I turned a corner, crossed a canal at full speed while crouching down to avoid being shot, and ran back to where I was staying. Once back, I noticed blood on my shirt and suddenly felt the pain from a wound on my hand. In the extreme excitement of running from the shooting, I had not realized I was hurt and did not know how or when it happened.

As far as I can determine, the foreigner who was shot near me was Ian Neumegen. While most sources say he was killed on May 19, I learned from his family that he was shot on May 18 at about 3 p.m., which would tally with what I had witnessed.

Many people were killed or injured during the Black May disturbances. Since Ian Neumegen was shot near me, I always felt some duty to note the specifics of his life. Ian was from New Zealand. He was 40 years old and had lived in Thailand for 12 years (some sources say 14 years). He assisted the Office of the Supreme Patriarch's Secretary and translated Buddhist works including writings by HRH the Princess Mother.

Gunfire went on continually around my neighborhood for the next five hours and then off and on throughout the night. While much of it might have been fireworks, there were times when something rattled down on the roof of my building.

V.

THE next day, the military clamped down around the city. Once an army starts openly shooting unarmed people on the street, there is really no need for further pretense or restraint.

From a balcony on my building, I watched government troops fire on motorcyclists near the bridge over Banglamphu Canal and witnessed small crowds taunting a line of soldiers advancing down Chakkra Phong Road.

Behind the first line of soldiers was a column of plainclothes soldiers carrying weapons — many military men masqueraded as civilians among the soldiers after the initial crackdown. The army was flaunting these plainclothes shooters on the streets as if to press home the point that people could not know who was an everyday person and who was a soldier in disguise. This was rumored from the beginning and I was warned not to trust anyone in the crowds.

After the earlier shooting, the protesters now taunting the soldiers were only the craziest young men, many riding pillion on motorcycles. Their weapon was potted plants that they threw at the soldiers. Potted plants sat at the front of nearly every shophouse by the dozen, so there was plenty of ammunition. All the while, buckshot or bullets were raining down on the roof of my building.

As they drew closer, the soldiers looked up and shouted at me (and probably others watching from other balconies on the building) and almost simultaneously peppered the structure with shot. I wondered if the soldiers would burst into my building and break down all the doors.

Groups of protesting motorcyclists numbering in the hundreds reportedly roamed the city, destroying government property and stopping traffic, one step ahead of the army. Later the next day, some opposition groups allegedly broke into gun shops and armed themselves — at least this was the story that was circulated.

That evening, some men on motorcycles, carrying weathered-looking weaponry and wearing bandannas over their faces, stopped along Samsen Road where people in the nearby market could get a look at them. Others appeared at the other end of the street as if to show they had captured the area. I just happened to be walking there when they arrived. They shouted slogans and carried a flag — the particular details of which one is not permitted to repeat, due to Thai law.

I knew what they were saying and was tempted to pull off one of their bandanas, but I became mesmerized by the non-reaction of the passing people. Everyone continued on as if the men in bandanas were not there. They were totally ignored. There was not a smirk or reaction of any kind from the shoppers, the merchants, or from men hauling produce. It was a truly bizarre spectacle, as the rough-hewn rebels shouted revolutionary slogans while every single person around them continued, almost robotically, with their tasks.

The masked men did not give any indication they were being ignored either. After a few more minutes and a couple more rounds of slogans, they sped away.

I asked a shop owner I was acquainted with what was going on. He was already laughing and chatting about it with a group of men.

"Those were soldiers," he said. "They are pretending to be radical protesters so they can say that the protesters were communists and it was ok to shoot them."

During this time, the government-controlled radio and TV stations showed the same programs as usual and occasionally had announcers come on air insisting everything was normal and that there was nothing unusual happening. This was while there was anarchy on the streets.

The Royal Hotel by Sanam Luang was old, sage, sprawling, and, like Thailand itself, had seen too much history. The hotel was trashed by soldiers who broke down its doors looking for protesters who had retreated there. A year later, I had my Thai-style wedding dinner at the hotel, adding some of my own personal ancient history to the place.

During Black May, I had to stay in my room for three days until the chaos subsided. The sound of gunfire erupted at all hours. There is nothing like hearing sporadic gunfire to keep one awake. I did not have a frame of reference for it. In my home country, I was taught to be alarmed over issues like zoning and trash pickup.

After the Thai king intervened with the famous televised admonishing of the parties involved, the tension went out of the situation. Suchinda resigned as prime minister and people started milling around the streets looking at bullet holes in the buildings, as the military retreated to its barracks.

Before Black May, Thailand was part of the Asian Tiger economic miracle of the region. The spectacle of protesters being shot in the streets, as well as the coup that preceded it was thought to be a thing of the past. Now these things were back again, brutal and present, reminding Thai people that nothing had really changed.

Society at large was aghast at the military's actions. As far as I could tell, there was little support for the military's solution to the impasse. As every Thai was quick to point out to me, shooting protesters — the disharmony of it — was not the Thai way. This was despite the fact that violence against protesters on the very same streets had been committed more than once in the past.

They did have a point that the Thai way was compromise. For those in power and those wielding power, deviation from the Thai way can have disastrous consequences. After the bravado of military rule and the hard line they took with the people, their retreat to the barracks and the release of the country from their grip must have been a bitter blow.

The death count was uncertain. The newspapers, publishing freely again, printed long lists of the missing. About 500 people were initially thought to be missing, perhaps killed and then secretly cremated by the military. The authorities said 40, but independent sources claimed it could be in the hundreds or even more. For those the military did admit were killed, bodies were never produced, nor exact details of their deaths. They simply vanished, just as the military did, back to its barracks.

I went to the trees along Ratchadamnoen Avenue where the military allegedly tied up protesters and executed them. People made the trees into makeshift shrines. Clearly, those "bloody trees" were staged. Four-day old blood is not bright red, and the soldiers, who were so meticulous in clearing away the remains of bodies, would not have missed a dozen bright-red trees.

Thais I knew countered that the trees were a military psy-ops campaign to create obviously faked death scenes in order to cast doubt on whether people were really shot on the streets. After all, the top military men had been trained in the U.S., they reasoned.

VI.

IN the wake of the violence, Anand was reinstalled as prime minister and implemented a number of confidence-restoring reforms for foreigners, such as work permits in 30 days and abolition of the notorious procedure that required foreign businessmen to buy places in line to bribe officials to get a tax certificate before leaving the country. Today, some foreigners are aware of corruption and may come into contact with it, but before Black May, the tax certificate system ensured every foreigner working in Thailand was intimately aware and complicit in bribing officials.

The events of Black May felt like the end of history at the time — the most consequential event imaginable that grabbed the throat of every person in the city. Soldiers marching, barbed wire, hectoring military men shouting from the TV, gunshots from those who carried guns directed at those who did not — all happening in the open.

So the people waited to see if anything could change. They waited to see if violence was the only true answer, but Black May is little remembered or memorialized. So many years have passed that it has receded, truly an event from last century. Even at the time, its context as a military power grab seemed old-fashioned in the wake of the end of the Cold War.

The resulting expectation of reform that was going to usher in an accountable, self-policing, democratic system also came and went. A "people's constitution" was drafted as a reaction to the events of Black May, and the political system it created began to morph into a new round of dictatorship, and then more coups and rounds of political conflict. Black May became a distant event with which it was impossible to draw direct parallels, and it was often grouped together with earlier instances of protest killings from the 1970s.

In later decades, these largely forgotten Thai massacres were revived and celebrated as part of a political drive by a billionaire who became prime minister and was himself deposed in a coup. While he was elected, he had as little desire to promote democracy as did the dictator Suchinda.

What little is written about Black May is in the autobiographies of the generals and politicians who lived through it and is usually along the lines of "I did the right thing, but I am very disappointed in everyone else."

As a U.S. taxpayer, one of the ways I saw Black May was as an example of weaponry and men, funded and trained in part by my tax dollars, being turned upon me. I suppose I knew such things happened, but it is a different thing to have that abstraction made reality. Then I really knew that on any day, soldiers could shoot people and just walk away. I pointed this out to my friends in Los Angeles who contended that police there should have "just shot" the rioters who looted Los Angeles in the weeks before Thailand's Black May. In the fullness of time, I grew to know that one cannot lose if one errs on the side of restraint and mercy.

I still feel the honor of having witnessed something historic during Black May, and, for a few years, my eye-witnessing meant something. There were usually Thai people at cocktail parties who wanted to assure the foreigners there about what really happened. The explanation was always that the protesters were student communists and that the military acted with self-restraint and did not shoot into crowds. I would then causally note that I had been there and saw what actually happened.

I took only five rolls of film during the disturbances. I thought it was a lot at the time. There was no internet and I never dreamed that there would be any use for snapshots — other than to take them out of a box and relive the events in the future. Today, the original developed prints look aged and yellow, as if they were from long, long ago.

For a few weeks after the shooting, Ratchadamnoen Avenue was littered with burned-out vehicles. Rumors circulated of yet another coup to reinstall Suchinda as prime minister. In the aftermath of Black May, I found myself jumping at sharp noises and thinking of those who had vanished.

Back at work, a lady whose father was known to be "highly placed," meaning a well-connected, high-born individual, gave a speech to the staff explaining that the soldiers were protecting Thai institutions from communists and that no one was shot. The other staff members were highly critical of her, and, in an unusual move for Thais, openly challenged her claims.

Later she confided to me that the younger staff at the school had been brainwashed by communists. When I told her I was an eyewitness to the shooting and confirmed that violence had taken place, she fell into a surprised silence. After I developed my photos, I tried to show them to her, but she refused to look.

UNDER SIAMESE SKIES

MALCONTENTS inevitably drifted west past the Mississippi into the freedom of what was once the Wild West. If that was not far enough, then it was on to California, then pushing farther west all the way to San Francisco. Some were driven on to the Golden Gate Bridge, jumping off when they could go no further.

Those with a passport and backpack escaped onward. Usually it was first to intimidating and frightfully organized Japan or to the moribund Philippines. The orderly Muslim nations of Malaysia and Indonesian were skipped, and Vietnam was unfriendly to the expat with its proud communism and its insane bureaucratic inhumanities. Cambodia was still a basket case emerging from genocide.

So finally it was Thailand.

Once there, only expensive, static-laden phone calls made at inconvenient times could connect one with home, incoming bank transfers took at least 45 days, and mail was sent on tissue-thin aerograms that took weeks to be delivered, if they arrived at all. It was blissful isolation for those who wanted it.

There was no more horizon to chase. India was expensive and uninviting, and the Middle East had yet to transform itself into a major business hub. The setting sun in the Andaman Sea was guarded by the unfriendly Burmese military. Burma (later Myanmar) was a fortress nation, second in its opacity only to the hermit kingdom of North Korea.

Thailand was the end for those who found themselves there. If what they wanted could not be had, there was nowhere further to go.

My office was in the oldest part of the city at the edge of Bangkok, nestled up against the Chao Phraya River as if I had chosen the western-most location as well. The traffic was thick, and to get to work, I had to run across a wide street where buses roared by and would not stop for anyone.

The neighborhood was suffused with exotic tradition. Huge golden Buddhas blocked foot traffic on the sidewalks. Temples nestled among modern cement buildings covered with moss. Alley after alley was stuffed with tiny shops selling food, spices and other exotic paraphernalia. It was a remote place even within the city. Each searching foreign soul could be completely alone with their thoughts. And we were.

The windows of the building I worked in were covered by a metal advertising façade. Random wires stretched behind the façade like black, tangled cobwebs and were covered with the dark dust that the city generated. Only bits of the buildings across the street could be seen through a few cracks.

I worked at a tutorial school and oversaw a small staff of foreigners who edited the publications the company produced. We non-Thais — the foreign staff — were segregated in our own room, as if it was unbearably uncomfortable for the Thais to be near us.

Initially the Thai owner of the company hired any foreigner who applied. He was not able to really judge one foreigner as being any more qualified than another. I suspected some of these hires were not even able to read — either by upbringing or mental illness. It seemed to me that he liked the strangest and most unqualified candidates more than the suitable ones.

I eventually wrested the authority to hire from him and he grudgingly admitted I might be a better judge of these strange foreigners than he was.

The drunk or oddball foreigner was tolerated in Thai businesses, because if a native English speaker was required, that was often all there was to hire. Thais, I think, assumed we were naturally weird. Perhaps we were. Engrossed in my solitude in the close foreign city, I had no way to really tell.

Ed, as I knew him then, was initially just another foreigner who I interviewed. I cannot recall his age then, but he appeared to either be a very old man or a young one who had aged terribly.

He had the hallmarks of a drinker: shaky and thin with a hungry look. As with so many searchers, he was moving ever onward, and, like all of us, his resume contained a variety of exotic-sounding countries where he had worked.

Ed was hired and we had spirited arguments over editing and linguistic issues each day. I can clearly recall long discussions on proper punctuation for lists of items and Ed denouncing "bastard words" — ordinals — in writing.

He wore oversized and rumpled clothes. Sitting in a brown padded office chair intently poised over his work, he looked like a long-legged insect. I admired his ability, despite his aged and frail appearance, to converse with the young foreign editors there as if he were a vibrant twenty-year-old born to argue his viewpoints with others.

Although vividly unkempt, he was a great intellect and could speak on many topics. He was the rare person I could talk with about the works of authors like Burroughs or Bukowski, who we both admired.

He was sometimes combative and almost petulant in the way he argued, maybe a symptom of being overemotional, but this just added to his distinctive character. He was, as we all were, a Bangkok eccentric.

Our Thai boss supplied us with pencils for editing and we were told they were special and expensive. They were blue and had soft leads that easily rubbed off on anything they touched. In the space of a day, Ed would become comically covered with pencil lead on the cuffs and sleeves of his shirt, and, most amusingly, all over his face. It symbolized to us the hard work of editing we were doing, as if we were miners getting covered with coal dust that proved our dedication.

Ed loved his money belt. This was a belt with a slit along the inside that money could be folded into for safekeeping. We were paid in cash on the last working day of the month, and I remember Ed taking off his belt and laboriously folding the bills to make them fit into his belt. It was like kneading dough, as he folded the bills lengthways and then mashed them into the belt until it was stuffed with all of that month's salary.

For some reason, the foreigners working there rarely asked each other anything more than what country they came from. Maybe it was because there was a sense that everyone who ended up in Thailand was burying themselves there for some reason. Maybe it was because we were so self-absorbed by our own dreams and failures.

I knew Ed was a special person who had no doubt permanently fled his own country. Years later, when access to all the world's knowledge became available via a search engine on a smart phone, I found that Ed was Edward A. Lacey, a noted poet and translator, who wrote the first book of gay-identified poetry published in Canada.

At the time, though, he was known as an old man who was rumored to hang around with young Thai guys. Not particularly unusual for Thai society, but probably not something that could be commonly engaged in back in his native country.

Eventually, a certain tempo ticked up in Ed. He was more irritable than usual. The normal arguments about English editing and usage conventions now ended with him saying, "Oh, never mind," and then refusing to talk more—sometimes sitting motionless in his chair for half an hour.

He was arriving at work even more disheveled, dirty, and later than usual, or sometimes not at all. More than once he claimed, unconvincingly, that someone had stolen all of his money. Despite this, our work was getting done and the Thais in management were completely unperturbed by weird behavior like this. No Thai saw anything wrong with the eccentric habits of the foreigners. It allowed each of us to be our own impenetrable secret.

Ed then missed work for three days, and when he finally returned, his face was cut and bruised and his eyeglasses smashed. They were taped up so he could still wear them, but at an angle so absurd that, at first glance, one might guess he was playing a joke by wearing them.

He said he had been beaten up, had spent time in the hospital, and lost his passport in the process. The local constabulary informed the company of the details of the case. The company and its bosses were important people in the area, so they were privy to news that concerned their employees. A Thai staff member pulled me aside and let me know of this police-supplied information. I was told matter-of-factly that Ed had a romantic entanglement with a young hustler and the problem was due to him not being able to pay for services rendered. He gave away his passport (easily sellable on the black market) as partial payment, but still got a beating. Plus, there was drinking by all involved.

This did seem to be a likely story, as Ed had told me about the multiple times he "lost" his passport in the past. In the fullness of these tales, it was revealed that he had a habit of drinking away his money and using his passport as a final asset to barter with.

Ed's bruised face healed, but he began hunching over his editing desk more than usual, as if not willing to see anything in his field of vision other than the document he was proofreading.

When we did talk after this incident, it was no longer about literature or editing, but just about what was happening with him. He talked of getting beaten up and beamed as if there was some misery in it that he enjoyed. He also suddenly despised everything in his home country and in Thailand with a passion. He had always been opinionated, but this was something more. The world was beginning to seem pointless to him.

The complaints he made about the venality and conformity of 1980s Canada and the U.S. were all true. His condemnation of the embarrassing and unacceptable corruption that Thailand tolerated was also valid. These were things that one had to look past or rationalize to be able to live. If a person saw all things clearly, it could kill them.

He had bouts when he was frantically searching for something he had misplaced around his desk. He would not (or could not) tell me what he was trying to find, but it irked him. He would gasp and sigh at the thing he had lost. Sitting there, face scarred, glasses broken, bone thin legs crossed and hunched over his work, he was contorted more than ever before.

The owner of the company we worked for regularly purchased movies on Laserdisc and showed them to his students. Before English-language captioning was available, a local company made little cartridges with English and Thai captioning and these fit in a companion device that synced them to the movie. The idea was that students might passively improve their English listening skills by watching the film and understanding the dialogue with help from the captioning.

We would also transcribe the dialogue from a movie and work it up into a script so that students could watch the film and read along with it which would presumably further their understanding.

This exhibition of films, which also went on in makeshift theaters in shopping malls where a small fee was charged, infuriated Hollywood film companies and local theater distributors, but the company I worked for had a permit that the police station had provided. This was posted at the door and made everything nice and legal, apparently.

My boss bought every film that was available, and, as a former cinema major in college, I relished the opportunity to see films that were otherwise impossible to view in Thailand. I sometimes stayed alone after work and watched these on the Laserdisc setup we used to transcribe the dialogue.

One day, the Laserdisc of *The Sheltering Sky* was sitting on my desk in preparation for viewing in the evening. This was the

Bertolucci-directed version of the classic Paul Bowles novel. Watching films was usually a solitary event for me, somehow even more delicious when I was ensconced in the solitude of this cement fortress in a faraway city.

Ed asked if I was going to watch the film that night and I told him I was. He had a jittery quality when something interested him and I could see he was anxious to see the film. He asked to stay and watch it, so that evening after work, we pushed our squeaky office chairs up to the TV.

Ed said nothing during the film, but afterwards he told me, "Thanks for very much for allowing me to watch this." He would sometimes pull himself together like this and speak in a sincere and formal way, as if he was peeking out of the chaos of everything around him to let someone know his true feelings.

Not only did we not speak any more about the film afterwards, but I felt myself avoiding even thinking about it. It was not a great film, nor a wholly successful one, but it captured some truth about people who needed to drift into vast deserts.

I was young, I thought. I still had time enough to succeed and be good enough, but this film was a prophecy, as was Ed himself. We both had moved to edge of the world. We had the temerity to abandon our culture. One could only be away for so long and something drains away so there is no longer a place of origin to get back to.

Then Ed had another bust-up the next month — another fight, a beating, and lots of alcohol.

He would not speak to anyone about it this time. His recently replaced glasses were again smashed and re-taped, and his face was bandaged. The embassy said there was nothing they could do — he was a grown man. He was a brilliant person. No one could intervene or reason him out of the path he was taking.

Every one of us was a bystander, passively hearing of the dangerous exploits, the alcoholism, and the panicked actions of others. To be involved risked getting swept into another's vortex of insanity. If there was one thing the expat wanted was to go down under his own distinct weight — weight accrued and borne privately. Sympathizing with another risked too much introspection about one's own march towards oblivion.

Ed was recharged, as though he was again enjoying whatever dangerous game he was playing, and, at the same time, was so consumed by dissatisfaction that he wanted something serious to happen.

I thought he wanted to die. I raised this with him, saying something like, "The way you are acting... Are you trying to kill yourself?"

He had a moment of irritation on his face, then reflection and then he shrugged it off.

"Who knows? Does it matter?"

"It does if you don't want to die."

"Does it matter?"

Maybe it does not after all, I thought. I was young and death was not real for me yet. It was a bad habit of others.

"Is there anything else?" he asked. "Is there anything else?" he repeated with annoyance. He knew I was out of things to say.

"No," I said.

It was a sentiment that passed distantly in the back of my mind then. At least I was a young man and had some chance, even if that chance was only more time.

Finally, Ed was absent again. It was not very surprising at this point.

Glass jars of Thai-style homemade whiskeys were sold on the sidewalks. Often they were fortified with pesticides or other proprietary mixtures of noxious chemicals to give a special high. It was easy for a person to become addicted to such easily obtainable and cheap liquor. For the alcoholically inclined, the concoctions could be instantly addicting, and Thais never dared to let on they thought anything was wrong with being continuously drunk. It was a dangerous free pass.

Fully half of my staff vanished on drinking binges after every payday. They returned after three to four days, more eager than ever to work hard so they could get to the next payday and have a drinking bout again. I had to insist that my boss not pay people weekly, as that meant each week I would have two or three days of no-shows after people were paid. Monthly pay guaranteed this would happen only once a month.

So I assumed another drinking bout, probably another fight.

After a week, Ed was still missing. Word got back to me that he had been drunk again and ran in front of a vehicle. Witnesses said it appeared that he had done it on purpose.

I visited him in the intensive care unit. The hospital had only a few lights on here and there, as if they were trying to save energy on lighting. There he was, trussed up, with hoses performing his various bodily functions.

His face was not injured this time, but his head was bandaged. This was what they called the "quiet ICU," where the head injury and coma cases were kept. There was no moaning and no obvious expressions of pain, just patients waiting for something mysterious in their brains to repair their consciousness.

I remember talking to Ed for a long time in hopes he was hearing me. I thought to myself, "He finally did it." He was called to death by some unfulfilled desire or alcohol or lack of love—all dumb, common things that will get us all. He had to kill himself here at the end of the world.

I visited several more times. Someone sent flowers. He once had his eyes open, but they were looking at nothing and did not move. I was just viewing the unconsciousness of a person I once knew—someone who was there and not there at the same time. It was an unforgettable truth. I always said, "Bye, Ed," many times as I left, retreating out of the ward as if I would not see him again.

Then one day I arrived and was told in the vaguest of terms that he had been returned to Canada with a metal plate in his head. There was no one I could contact about it. Then it all drifted away. I forgot the names of the others I worked with as they came and went.

In Bangkok, the evening light was dim and yellow, like something scary was about to happen. I was just a person living paycheck to paycheck. It was just enough that, over time, I lived with my head down, moving fast, and not thinking too much. I would get used to it.

The years passed. I had very little. I took the bus home in the rain day after day. I walked through cold puddles on my way to see my girl. My pants cuffs were soaked and I was chilled by the time I saw her.

One Sunday I needed to go to an old shopping center for some reason. I cannot recall why. I walked through the musty mall and saw that the main shops had gone out of business and were shuttered. Tables were set up in the main open atrium of the mall where women were trying to sell mounds of clothes. It was dark except for makeshift lighting — bare bulbs — over each of the tables selling clothes. I was struck by a dread I had never felt before.

There are many depressing places in the new Asia. Legions of concrete buildings pressed in on mosques or Buddhist temples. Concrete stamped with black mold or lichen or exhaust. Cement works, quarries, giant complexes of unknown machines, slash and burn farming — all things that produced dust and smoke. It was raw industry that required toil and workers from other places, from farms gone dry, working faithfully, holding their minds to the inevitability of the myths of their land that demanded people do the right things. All obediently going to and from work as instructed, selling their family's land to buy pickup trucks, living hand to mouth.

Yet all of that lifted people up, I was told. The expanses of roads and condos and tourism and factories fueled growth, which was money that grew tall buildings and long bridges. It was long needed. I guess it was — after all, I was fetishizing the old, poor, and exotic East and knitting it into my own fears. It was too big for me to comprehend and understand.

As my novelty unfurled and became an unbroken pattern of work days and weekends, it began to weigh on me. This vague oppression created an identification with the blank-faced workers and the randomness of life — the lost daughter, the death by motorcycle or jealous lover, the news of broken bodies splashed on the front pages of the vernacular dailies. News of foreigners just like me felt even keener — morgue shots on the front page of newspapers, dead eyes open in stark terror. It was coming from a way of life I never knew before nor dreamed of, yet I was now living.

I was just one of the fools at the mercy of circumstance in a far-off land, unable to grasp the life I expected to have. What had set me apart from this before was that I was young and had time. Now that time had passed, the truth was rushing up to me.

I sometimes wondered what became of Ed or if there was anything more that could have happened to him. Over twenty years later I discovered an extensive biography of him, aptly entitled *Lost Passport*. Ed lived an unbelievable and mostly ill-advised life in many exotic places, but he was returned to Canada as an invalid, did recover a bit, but finally died of a heart attack, aged 57.

SEEING THE COMET

WHEN I was a young boy, I stood in the far corner of my yard night after night waiting to see a comet. As the rain poured down, I gripped my notepad full of childish science notes as it became soggy. A comet was a rare thing to see so far outside of the world of a little kid like me. I wondered about comets and what it would mean to really see one.

My family scoffed. It had been raining week after week. It was always cloudy, so why even bother? It was a waste of time. This was just another one of the odd things I was always doing.

I was hoping that the clouds would clear for an instant and I would see that thing I was waiting for. It was a comet for all to see. It must mean many things as it zoomed through the sky.

Appearing is the beginning of ending and it must be seen, even if through clouds and pouring rain.

"Did you know that in the olden days people thought a comet was a warning of coming doom?" someone in my family volunteered. Yes, I knew that.

On one night it was finally clear. I rushed out and found the place in the sky, but the thing I could see was just a smudge. It was only a vague white cloud that I would never have otherwise noticed. It looked nothing like the extravagant comet illustrations showing star-like objects with long, curved, bright tails, zooming overhead.

Defeated, I went back inside to watch TV. It was cartoons and occasionally news of inflation and the expected decline of my country.

****

BIRDS of the species *Aerodramus fuciphagus* build nests by excreting saliva which hardens into little half cups that are cemented to cave and cliff walls. Slender bamboo scaffolding is set up to harvest the nests. The nests are then canned and sold for high prices as a delicacy, sometimes touted as having curative powers. It is among the world's most expensive foods.

The nests are found in the Thai south. This is the realm of both Muslim villagers as well as the Moken, a native sea people. One might assume that a tribe with access to such a lucrative resource would be rich, but tribal peoples rarely get to benefit from the resources of their own land. These sea people are disenfranchised paupers, worse off because they happened to possess such a valuable boon.

Far away in Bangkok, businessmen look after the precious birds' nests for the sea people and auction off the rights for collection and sale for colossal sums for the good of the nation.

I was driving down the Malay Peninsula to bring a car to my boss, who was somehow involved in one of those bird's nest projects, taking care of the valuable resources since the sea people could not be trusted with it. He had earlier flown down and was working on the deal, but had decided that having his giant Mercedes to drive around would help in affirming his status in the negotiations.

The car was an outsized squarish tank, a gigantic, mid-1990s S-class Mercedes Benz. It was a tight, stable driving machine, despite its dimensions. It also had incredible shocks and I liked to hit potholes and other bumps at full speed. The car barely registered them.

The 1990s S-class was, and long remained, a singular vehicle, as its size instantly set it apart from all other cars. It screamed that those inside, even in that German utilitarian automobile, must be experiencing a decadent ride and must be those who could afford drivers take them where they wanted to go.

Such a car perfectly fit the spectacular economic growth of the region, of which Thailand was a beneficiary. Lines of these massive Mercedes idled outside of department stores, drivers waiting as their newly wealthy owners shopped inside. Every tradition was expected to soon be supplanted by the preeminence of money. The power and influence of the old would be taken over by a new class driving Mercedes. Every direction was up and the car signaled that.

I did not know why I was told to drive the car down instead of one of my boss's Thai workers. I guessed it was probably because there was added status in my boss showing he had a foreign employee, but during the trip, I never ended up meeting anyone connected with the bird's nest deal.

Usually in a Thai company, if one does not say something is "urgent," it means the task does not have to be done at all. In this instance, the boss told me it was indeed urgent that I get the car to him right away. He began calling at least hourly, asking why the car was not there already.

I was provided the company's then novel and bulky Motorola flip, an early cell phone. The signal was in and out, and most areas had no coverage, but I quickly realized why I had been given the phone. Although the boss knew very well the car would not be there in one or two or even three hours after I left Bangkok, he called anyway, and his petulant needling made me know it was important that the boss get his car as soon as possible.

I was met with kilometers of bumpy and patched sections of road, deep holes marked only by palm fronds stuck in them as a warning, and the occasional buffalo or elephant being herded along the highway. Thick dust swirled from both the decaying road and the ceaseless construction at every roadside town during that boom time.

Eventually, it would become hard to see, and the car's wipers only smeared grit across the windows. Then I would have to stop and wipe the grime away.

Typical of the roads of the day, the highways were terribly maintained. Once a new road was planned, all maintenance ceased on the old one, even if the new road was years away. The road signs were in a foreign language to me, and even then, they were sometimes contradictory. It was easy to get headed in the wrong direction.

The trip was a diversion from my routine in Bangkok where I was nestled in among the buildings, going to work, coming home, and doing my laundry on the weekends. It was a routine like this that I had tried to escape from by coming to Asia in the first place, and here I was, stuck in the same life, so far away from where I had started.

It might have been a mistake moving away from my country. It was turning into a decade of career stall for me in a place where most jobs were off limits. I was missing the dot-com boom and never bought a house. Getting locked into a lifetime mortgage was considered the thing every normal person did where I was raised, along with having children and amassing credit card debt.

So, just as anyone who stalls in their career and prospects, I did what they all do — got married. Nothing like marriage to fool one into thinking he is making progress in his life when nothing is happening.

I was no more successful at that, and I learned how keenly it felt to perplex my wife with my moods and uncertainty about the present and the future that drew me ever inward.

Just being in Bangkok was dislocating. It was living in a way I was not programmed for — all the while nurturing a growing sense of dread. Disappointing her.

I heard the stories about foreigners who moved to Thailand, married a local girl and become part of the local economy — farming rice and then drinking whiskey during the off-season. Then, without realizing it, their fortunes dwindled and they grew poorer and poorer. No longer able to travel or have the choice of what they wanted to do, they ended up with long-expired visas, saving up money for the rare trip into town to shop, and dying from liver trouble. It was a seduction by acceptance and the ease of living — a thousand expats pursuing their lonely hobbies.

Yet there was eventually a time, different for every foreigner, when it became unbearable to leave. I heard about some neurotic foreigner who ran his visa out and refused to leave the island he was staying on. He was carried off kicking and screaming. Foreigners facing having to go back to their cold homelands had been known to try to kill themselves at the airport while waiting for their flights.

I had thought that travel — going really far away — would allow me to realize something. Now I was not sure what I needed to realize.

At that time in all of history, the Hale-Bopp Comet was approaching my planet. I read something about it being among the brightest comets in human history and it sat vaguely in my mind, but I had given up hope of seeing comets long ago.

After a few more kilometers, the car started to shake and then the right front tire shredded off the rim, most of it hurtling up in a long frayed ribbon over the car, leaving a long scrape on the hood as it flopped down. I stopped and jacked up the car and got the old shredded tire off. The spare was in the trunk and properly inflated, but when I got it out, it was not the right size tire that would fit the car.

I was in between towns with no phone signal, finally at a dead standstill. The road in either direction was nearly empty. In subsequent decades, huge service stations were built along Thailand's highways, but in those days, only small local gas stations existed and they were inside towns. One needed to calculate that there was enough gas to get to the next town and then make sure to get more before going onwards.

The surrounding horizon wavered in the hot sunlight. I was in for a long wait or a long walk. Losing any time was not going to be acceptable.

Then movement slowly became visible in the far distance. It flickered in the rising heat from the roadway. At first all I saw was a brown fluttering tail of dust, but then it resolved into single motorcyclist thundering down the wrong side of the empty divided highway right at me. The dust formed a swirling crescent behind him.

Finally, the motorcyclist arrived, as if I had summoned him. He was an old sinewy man who looked like he was most at home on his motorcycle. He gestured for me to get on.

I hooked the massive dud tire on the back of the motorcycle seat and we were off, back the way he had come. I had no idea where I was going, but at least we were going somewhere. We went a long way, seeing only a few trucks rumbling along in the opposite direction. Then we turned down a small side road and eventually came to a gas station that stood alone amid dry fields.

It looked closed, but a single person sat out near two gas pumps. The motorcyclist said something to the person and we walked into the large empty garage of the station. On a wall were rows of racks for holding tires.

On the top row at the far side was a single tire. The gas station man slid a tall ladder over and went up and grabbed the dust-covered tire. Amazingly, this last tire, the only tire in the shop, was the right one. The man cut the old tire off the hub and then deftly eased the new tire on with a crowbar and soapy water and then inflated it.

He grabbed a toolbox and followed us on his motorcycle back to the Mercedes.

In a moment, the tire was back on the car. I paid the mechanic and the old motorcycle man who rescued me. I cannot recall what the old man asked for, but I remember it was a ridiculously low amount. I gave him more, although that still did not seem to be enough.

I was able to partially buff out most of the scrape the floundering tire had made on the hood and what was left of it would probably go unnoticed for now. I had to get back on the road. I was frantic to make up time, but it was a strangely nice feeling to have affirmed that things do work out and that the omens were good for me.

Later in the day, I was roaring up a hill. At the peak, a boy and his dog suddenly darted across the road from right to left. The dog was several steps ahead and well into the road when a huge truck going the opposite direction came careening down the hill. It hit the dog, narrowly missing the boy, who had yet to enter the highway. The dog literally exploded into fragments and a shower of blood was flung across the road. I can still see the poor dog's long narrow head twirling around and around and sailing over the Mercedes, spattering a stream of blood across the hood and windshield. The boy halted at the edge of the road, regarding the scene with no expression. I hoped he was not too traumatized by what he saw. I did not even slow down. The truck zoomed on in a noisy cloud of dust. It happened in a second and there was no way I was going to stop with the boss calling every hour. Then I was kilometers away.

I stopped in a parking lot and dabbed off the blood. I was beginning to be influenced by the lore and superstitions of the land and I knew that any news of this rain of blood over the car would be seen as an evil portent. It weighed on my own mind as a sign of coming bad luck, and I had to firmly put it out of my mind, telling myself not to be influenced by unscientific beliefs.

I finally met the boss at a remote hotel on the Krabi coast along the Andaman Sea. This was one of Thailand's most spectacular settings, with towering limestone cliffs alternating with beaches. The expansive hotel was in one of the gaps between limestone cliffs on the seaside.

The boss was in an intense and distracted mood, and, like the executive types I worked for both in Thailand and the U.S., was unwilling or unable to isolate his emotions. When something was going wrong — like the negotiations for the bird's nest concession — it meant that it was necessary to find fault with everything and see everything in the most negative light.

Thus, there was some grumbling, first about why I took so long to get there and then that the car was dusty and not washed (to make a good impression on those he would meet). It was lucky he did not know about the dog blood incident.

His grumbling was just pettiness on his part, but it revealed to me that the negotiations were not going as planned. It also showed that he felt comfortable enough to openly complain to me about anything and everything. I knew to just reply as little as possible and it would soon be forgotten, as the moods of such people turn by the day.

I barely had a chance to grab my overnight bag out of the car before he jumped in and sped away without another word, leaving me to a lone gruff attendant who escorted me through the deserted lobby of the hotel. It was not possible to tell whether the hotel was just about to open or was just about to close.

I was shown to my room far down an impossibly long hallway. The doors of many of the rooms along the way were open. Some were in the process of construction. Others were being furnished.

I guessed that this must be a complex owned in part by my boss or one of the men he was negotiating with — a hopeful investment meant to capitalize on the tourism boom which was assumed to be never-ending. Every family with a piece of land they could leverage for financing was building something. Often they ran out of funds to continue the project and could only continue building very slowly. This must have been what this hotel was.

There were many buildings like this in Thailand, started with iffy financing and left half-finished or half-occupied, limping along in hopes that building it would create profits which could be used to finish the construction.

It was nearly the end though. The Thai government's financial ineptitude was poised to spark a currency contagion that would spread around the world and definitively end the conceit that Asia could grow forever. The kingdom would soon become littered with abandoned, half-finished "ghost buildings" when the Asian financial crisis started in Thailand just a few months later. Jobs evaporated and street after street of businesses were shuttered overnight. Every person was shocked that the good times did not go on forever, uninterrupted.

Once at the door of my room, I watched the attendant walk back down the unfinished hall like he was walking into infinity. I marveled that anyone would make a hallway that long. It was a bold attempt to cram in as many rooms and envision the rosiest future possible, when untold numbers of tourists would clamber to throw their money at the country.

It was already growing dark, and, from the window of my room, I saw the stark limestone cliffs that bordered the hotel grounds. The sky beyond was only slightly lighter, creating a delicate line between the darkness of the sky and the cliffs.

The phone in the room did not work and there was no mobile signal. I was sure I was pretty much alone in the hotel that night.

This was the realization of what I had aimed for when I first decided to travel outside of my own country—being alone, far away, out of sight and mind of every person who I ever knew, hopefully forgotten. It was a strange bliss to achieve this. There was no way to go any further.

Little bottles of alcohol were lined up in the mini-bar. I regarded them. They were golden and delicate and enticing. Even in a half-finished hotel, no room would be complete without tempting me with this blissful delicacy. They might as well also supply sleeping pills or a gun.

I exited the hotel and saw my room had the only light on in the building besides the lobby. Walking aimlessly, I could soon hear the concussive splash of the waves. I went right up to the sea— refreshing, filthy, dangerous, immortal. Statues were placed along the beachside. They were Thai mythological creatures: *kinnaree*— half-female, half-bird creatures who watch, angel-like, over mankind—standing and smiling for no one—as well as a *yaksha*, a sort of demon who harried and confused travelers.

To my right, I spied a flight of zigzagging stairs that led up the side of the limestone cliffs that hemmed in the area. Without a moment's thought, I headed directly to them and started climbing.

It was dark and I felt my way up the stairs. Instead of being sheer cliffs as they looked from the ground, the limestone tilted away and the stairs began to move across a dome-like mound of rock with its peak just over the horizon.

I despaired of the darkness — it was getting so I could not see at all. I wondered if the stairs were in disrepair and would drop me down a deep dark hole, but I had already come this far and continued to feel my way along.

I kept going and soon was able to perceive that I was coming to the last flights of stairs. Then I rose above the tops of the cliffs and into view sprang the most magnificent and unexpected sight I ever beheld. It was a comet — the Hale Bopp Comet. It was a bright eternal comet with a fuzzy head and long spectacular tail. I had seen nothing like it in the sky before or since — white oil paint on a blue-black background exploding in an impossible rocket-like blast.

My boss never closed his deal and flew back to Bangkok, but it was ok. I had finally seen a comet. It would soon pass this world, forever going forward. I drove the car back to Bangkok. There was no hurry this time. Every kilometer was easier than the last, and I knew if I ended up stopped on the road, I would not have any trouble getting back.

It was the brightest in human history, they said.

IT REMAINS THERE

IN the earliest days, I was alone. Each morning I sat in the lobby of my guesthouse and read every word of the *Bangkok Post* — every word, every advertisement, with a mantra-like dedication, as if to fill the unknown time I had entered into.

The Thai-language newspapers contained much more information than the English-language ones — I could tell. There were photos of political figures, news of gruesome accidents, and oceans of Thai-language script — tiny, inscrutable, geometric, and infinite in its regularity across page after page, like the stitching of some kind of fabric.

The din and confusion and bigness of everything was not about me. It made for a pleasantly bracing and distracted life. I would find a way of achieving in this world — I was sure of that.

Sometimes girls would eat lunch with me in the modest guesthouse restaurant and teach me Thai phrases while motorboats screamed down the canal next to the building. The sound rattled the windows and bit into my finely tuned sense of what was offensively loud. Each time the boat passed, it created in me an indignant anger rising at the noise, but the Thai girl simply paused, smiled as the sound rattled us both, and then went on with her explanations of the Thai language. Eventually, I too grew immune.

I even got used to seeing a lady on the other side of the canal emptying her daily trash slowly into the waters, laboriously drowning each floating tissue with a stick.

****

AT the turn of the century, I began working for an international company located in the cosmopolitan business district of Bangkok. This was finally a living wage and I no longer had to choose between taking a bus and buying a Coke. I was then forever far away from the grit and the occasional magic of the faithful, reverent Thais, and instead, more often at chamber of commerce cocktail parties with corpulent white people who rarely left air-conditioning surroundings.

The region changed too. One day, the forests of Cambodia were impassible with ruined bridges and banditry and I was hiding from the Khmer Rouge. The next day, it seemed, I was zooming across fresh and smooth roads in a tour van from Thailand to Cambodia as if I was off to visit a beach in Florida.

In the new century, there would no longer be any funny business like crossing unmarked frontiers on a motorbike, being in a country without a visa, working illegally, walking through customs in airports with the influential to buy duty-free alcohol, or facilitating a briefcase of money from a certain avionics company... and there are still other tales too dangerous to tell. I am not admitting to any of that—just that it would no longer be possible as times became too civilized and I became unaccountably fearful.

Back in the twentieth century, I would sit in a quiet, sparse hotel room — maybe in Hanoi or Yangon — no TV or phone, just looking out over a hazy alien city. There was no news, but only the indefinable text of the local language, further obscured by the censorship of each culture. It was a bliss that I did not know would soon be forever lost. Today few places are out of contact. Few places exist where every human does not have a phone with a camera at the ready.

My fearless days passed and only now do I see how dangerous and precious they were. While I was once rock solid when facing danger, now I tremble when I get the mail. Will a tax collector bedevil me? Do I have enough money? Is the paperwork correct? The fleeting highs of youth have given way to the neurosis and grinding worries and stomach fat of age.

I can still hear my wife — as any Thai would — gently and matter-of-factly assign her upcoming death from cancer to karma — meaning actions she had taken in a previous life. They are all gone now — her grandparents, her parents, and her. After only a few decades, I outlived them all. Their memories were handed off to a foreign man who could never really understand them, but I hold on to their time and their stories while I can.

The ghosts that once visited me, my failures, and the luck of a young man are receding. They drifted away so imperceptibly that I barely noticed.

So in this little window of time, I have written down my adventures and follies so someone will know what I witnessed and that I was grateful for it. It was when I could go ever outward in all the time I ever had — in all the time there is.

A storm is blowing in now and the distant revving of motorcycles, once jarring, has become comforting. After the rain, the air will smell of the smoke used to heat a thousand breakfast stoves. Then the sun will return to shine on every part of this world.

Ron Morris, Củ Chi, Vietnam, circa 1990

RON MORRIS is a writer, political analyst, and traveler.

BOOKS BY RON MORRIS

MATTER OF A THING ABSOLUTE

EDGE OF THE GOLDEN MOON

IN A COUNTRY WITH NO NAME

THERE ARE STILL UNKNOWN PLACES

LAST CENTURY

THE THAI BOOK: A FIELD GUIDE TO THAI POLITICAL MOTIVATIONS